Kulkuri (Vagabond) and Other Short Stories
By Mark Munger

Cloquet River Press
Publishing Stories from the Lake Superior Basin
www.cloquetriverpress.com

First Edition
Copyright 2019, Mark Munger

All rights reserved, including the right to reproduce this book or any portions thereof, in any form, except for brief quotations embodied in articles and reviews without written permission of the publisher. The opinions, observations, and references herein are those of the author alone.

These stories are fiction. Places, characters, organizations, or incidents are products of the author's imagination and are used fictitiously. Any resemblance or reference to "real" people, places, organizations, living or dead, is used by the author as part of the artistic license inherent in a fictional tale. Quotations used are from the film *Revolutionary Road* (2008. Paramount) and were transcribed by the author after multiple viewings of the movie. Any inaccuracies in transcription are wholly unintentional.

ISBN 978-1-7324434-1-9
Library of Congress Number: 2019901785
Published by: Cloquet River Press
                5353 Knudsen Road
                Duluth, Minnesota 55803
                (218) 721-3213
Edited by Ms. Betsey Norgard
Photo by Mark Munger (Wirtanen Farm: Makinen, Minnesota)
Visit the Publisher at: www.cloquetriverpress.com
E-mail the Author at: cloquetriverpress@yahoo.com
Printed in the United States of America

ACKNOWLEDGMENTS

I would like to thank the following individuals who served as readers for this project: Vicky Hubert, Patricia McNulty, Jeff Velline, Donna Salli, and Ron McVean.

Without these dedicated friends devoting their time and effort to reading the manuscript, the content and flow of these stories might be vastly different and—more than likely—vastly inferior.

A word of thanks to my wife, René. Many days and nights have been lost to family while I type away at the keyboard, struggle with revisions, or sleep in my chair because I've been up at five in the morning working on this book. Her patience through the duration of this project is much appreciated.

Finally, this collection was written over a considerable period of time. Most of these stories have never seen the light of day before being published in this format. However, "Isle Royale" was selected for inclusion in *The Thunderbird Review,* an anthology of local writers published by Fond du Lac Tribal College. "Brule River, Minnesota" was awarded second place in the 2019 Northwestern Ontario Writers Workshop writing contest. "Threshold" was the winner of a Lake Superior Writers short fiction writing contest sometime in the distant past. The other stories and the novella are being seen, and hopefully read, by readers for the very first time. I hope I got it right.

Mark Munger
2020
Duluth, Minnesota

Table of Contents

Brule River	11
Kulkuri (Vagabond)	17
Hemingway's Mistress	24
The Angle: A Novella	29
Threshold	107
Isle Royale	114
Hannibal's Elephants	122
Rain	126
Katydid	132
Crazy	141
The Last Jew	149

Tell me the truth, Frank, remember that? We used to live by it. And you know what's so good about the truth? Everyone knows what it is however long they've lived without it.
April Wheeler
(Revolutionary Road)

For René and the boys ...

Kulkuri (Vagabond) and Other Short Stories

Brule River

I stand thigh deep in the cold embrace of the Brule seeking forgiveness. God does not answer my prayer. The only sound I hear is the rushing of black water against hip waders. You'd think I'd know better. Talk to God? I've ignored Him for the better part of my adult life though, in times like these, times when I'm troubled and sinking in a trough of despair, I've been known to look to Heaven for answers. But despite serious petitions to the Almighty, no whispers of salvation reach my ears. The gurgling of water across neoprene, stones, and deadfall; the river's subtle voice accompanied by the distant cawing of crows—irritated at my intrusion into their woody sanctuary—is all I hear inside the gabbroic canyon surrounding me.

It isn't her fault, I think, drawing the tip of a Fenwick bamboo rod—an artifact from my father—towards me in anticipation of sending a wet fly towards a deep hole where I suspect a brook trout, a legendary fish, a big female—its sides bursting with the colors of the rainbow—is lurking. The fly sheds dollops of water as it passes my right ear. I take up slack in the floating line and cast the artificial bait across the pool. The fly lands where the river's pulse bleeds into calm water. This presentation will allow the lure to waltz downstream at the river's cadence such that a hungry brookie will be unable to resist it. *She never asked me to do it,* I think, unable to ignore the trouble that has brought me to seek respite in wilderness.

I'm an officer in a bank, the Consolidated Bank of Two Harbors. I got my job, vice-president and supervisor of the bank's trust and investment department, after earning a bachelor's degree in business from the University of Wisconsin-Superior. Not many decent jobs were open to a guy with a BA when I graduated. Until I married right. Cynthia Leppela, the girl I married, the woman I'm married to, was the right one. Cindy isn't only attractive; she's also athletic, having been a pitcher on the Agates' softball team and the goalie on the girls' soccer team. She's kept her figure through three pregnancies and still, at thirty-eight—our attempts at procreating having ended prematurely due to a weak cervix, two miscarriages, and tied fallopian tubes—she remains a looker. Short. Compact. High cheekbones. Ample lips. Slight of bust. Wide hipped. Raven hair and platinum blue eyes: a stunning combination of her Italian mother and her Finnish father.

As I wait for a fish to strike, I envision my wife standing in her nightgown looking lovingly into Claire's crib. Moonlight filtering through a window allows a suggestion of my wife's breasts, her tummy, her hips, and her legs beneath the gauze of her gown as she watches our only child. Claire is snoring away. A smile creeps across my weary face as I watch the tip of the Fenwick rod twitch.

I've tried to be the best husband, lover, and provider I can be, I muse as the fly ends its drift. I retrieve fluorescent green line with my right hand, the excess coiling and floating on the water's surface around my waders. When all the line is in, the leader and fly hang from the rod tip. I re-cast, confident that the fly will drift past a half-submerged log. I'm certain that's where my hypothetical trophy is lurking. The fish is likely suspended inches above the river's gravel bottom, resting in shadow, waiting in ambush. *I knew better. I knew that Cindy wouldn't ask me to cross that line to make her happy. And yet, somehow, I want to blame her.*

It was wrong from the start. I knew it then. I know it now. You can't sugarcoat the truth so I won't. But my intentions, if one goes back and revisits what I was thinking two years ago, weren't as dishonorable as they now appear. I'm not trying to excuse my actions. I'm just trying to explain why I did what I did.

I truly believed I was only borrowing money. At least, that's how I sold the deed to myself when I found we were short of cash and unable to keep up with the bills that owning two quarter horses—pure blooded and papered and outfitted with the best tack money can buy—entails.

I could live without the horses. We own animals on account of my wife. It's not that I don't ride. I've had some good times astride Buster—the big red roan gelding Cindy says is "my" horse. Buster, like Cinnamon—the buckskin mare Cindy usually rides—is really my wife's horse, not mine. But the problem isn't the animals; they're both easy going, fine looking, good-natured stock. It's the cost of owning them. With no barn or hayfield or corral on our property, boarding two horses, especially horses meant for competition, isn't cheap. And despite Cindy's pronouncement that she needed five grand to buy Buster for *me*, she's the only one who's ridden Buster in her quest for ribbons and prize money. Just last summer, she won the Lake County Fair barrel race riding Buster. Add to Buster's price tag the seven grand we forked over for Cinnamon, the horse Cindy has ridden to victory in other events, and you can see how things add up. What with boarding fees, hay, feed, veterinarian bills, and the like, not to mention the expense of a reliable pickup truck and the cost of a durable horse trailer, I'm sure you get the picture. Such expenses are impossible to afford on a banker's salary; even a salary negotiated with a father-in-law who understands his daughter's needs.

Lester Kinnunen is an old Finnish bachelor who once owned and ran the local hardware store. When his nephew proposed buying the business, Lester hammered out a pretty sweet deal for the kid. The money Lester received as a down payment for the building and inventory wasn't earth shattering—just a hundred grand. But that amount, coupled with the monthly payments the kid pays Lester, add up. So the old Finn came to me to make sound, conservative investments for him. Which is what I did. Until our bills caused me to embezzle from Lester's account.

A bald eagle glides through the canyon. Sunlight strikes the white head and tail of the great bird with dazzling clarity. The eagle cries. I feel a tug. The floating line becomes taut but I'm not ready to set the hook. *Take it.* My father, an ex-Marine and dead for years, taught me the patience of waiting on trout. I follow his example as current swirls around the glistening line connecting the bamboo rod to what I hope is a legendary fish, a fish I can mount on my bank office wall.

I'd intended to borrow a smidgen from Lester's investment account; just a small loan to see us through a rough patch. There's no way Cindy would've approved my deception even though she's accustomed to a certain standard of living. Cindy's someone her father never said "no" to. I understand why. She was, like Claire, an only child, a spoiled child. Not by way of attitude but by way of entitlement. But while Cindy's never gone without, I know her mettle. My wife could, if worse came to worse, tighten her belt and sell Buster if need be. Hell, she'd sell both horses and everything else that means anything to her before doing what I did.

But I did not want to disappoint the woman I love. It's pretty clear to me—and everyone who knows us—that Cindy is *way* out of my league. I'm bearded, short, rotund, and balding; not at all what women like Cindy usually deem to be "a catch." Yet something clicked between us. She said it was my brown eyes and impish grin and my ribald humor that drew her in. Maybe. Or maybe I remind Cindy of her old man. There's a certain physical resemblance between us, and like I said, we do share a vocation.

In the beginning, I borrowed only a few grand from Lester's account and kept things on the down low by having two sets of books; one set being the actual ledger of Lester's investments and the other memorializing my debt to the old Finn. My first sin kept us in the black for three months. Then the Ford blew a head gasket and Cindy needed to buy a new pickup truck and I didn't have the heart to say no. Over the course of two years, my debt to Lester grew to fifty grand.

Lester came into the bank yesterday to say he wants to cash out. He met an Estonian woman—Etta Tuka—a stunner fifteen years his junior, on the ferry between Helsinki and Tallinn. The two of them hit it off. There's going to be a wedding in Varnja, the Estonian village Etta calls home located on the west shore of Lake Peipus. There's talk of the two of them buying an apple orchard and living near Varnja happily-ever-after. Lester and I agreed he'll come in to close out his account on Monday. It's Saturday afternoon. I have two days to come up with Lester's cash but that's not gonna happen.

The floating line has disappeared. I set the hook. "Christ!" Immediately, I'm impressed by the weight and the power of the fish. The brookie is indeed a trophy. It's late September. The leaves are turning. The mornings are cool and the days are growing shorter. Come the first of October, stream trout season will close and brook trout will spawn uninterrupted by fishermen. "This is the biggest brookie I've ever had on," I whisper. The fish jets down river. I maintain steady pressure on the line but I don't force the trout to go anywhere she doesn't want to go.

To make things worse, Erik "Bud" Leppela—my father-in-law and boss—has been poking around. Normally he lets me do my thing but for some reason his interest has been piqued. There's also an audit coming up. Last year I avoided trouble by sleight-of-hand accounting. But that trickery won't work a second time. Maybe the new truck is what tipped Bud off. Or, the opal necklace, earrings, and bracelet I gave Cindy for Christmas were a catalyst for suspicion. That was stupid—an extravagant gesture. But God, I love that woman. She deserves to be treated like a queen, what with all she's been through. She gave up teaching, gave up coaching, gave up everything (except the horses), and endured two failed pregnancies before becoming a mom to Claire. I know she loves me. But that's gonna change. Once the shit hits the fan, she'll wash her hands of me. Cindy's tough as nails. She can tolerate a lot. We survived the one mistake I made during our marriage, the one involving Jeanie. Never slept with that girl. But it was close. That little misunderstanding took months to smooth over. Had I slept with Jeanie Franklin, a twenty-seven-year-old, newly-divorced teller at the bank, well, that would have done us in. But this is worse. Honor. The family name. Small town prominence. All these mean a lot to Cynthia. *I am so screwed.*

I sense the trout tiring. I try to relax, exhaling as if to expel demons. Despite my angst, the beauty of this rugged place, where ebony water rushes over ancient volcanic rock, is not lost on me. Even as I consider what will happen on Monday, I take note of the fish tugging at the end of my line, of the bluebird sky, of the forest slowly turning in season, and of the sunshine warming my face. These things remind me of what I have. What we have. I test the line. The fish is winded. I crank the open-faced reel, its mechanical "click" at odds with the subtle voice of the river. And then, she's swimming next to me, her tail methodically waving in the current.

"Holy shit!"

I tuck the butt of the fly rod under my left arm and reach into the water with bare hands. I lift the scarlet and blue and yellow speckled fish, her fins streaked with the same white that graced the head and tail of the departed eagle, free of the water's embrace. I hoist three pounds of tired brook trout into cooling air as the sun slips behind a rocky escarpment. The brookie struggles in my wet hands, and for a moment, I fear I'll drop her. But I don't. I consider the trout and decide that the would-be trophy must be released. I remove the hook from the fish's upper lip, bend over, and gingerly hold the big fish in current. Water rushes through her gills. She regains her strength and I let her go. I do this because she's a coaster; a female brook trout heavy with eggs who's left the big lake to spawn in the river. Her fins flash white against the inky water and, with a swipe of her broad tail, she disappears.

I catch a half-dozen other trout. None are longer than ten inches. I consider these wild, native fish and their will to survive as they too vanish upon release. Ruefully, I contemplate the Browning .45—another artifact from my father—fully loaded and stuffed into the glove compartment of the Toyota FJ Cruiser I parked a mile downstream. *That's one way of avoiding Monday,* I think as I secure the fly to an eyelet of the old rod before stepping free of water.

I leave the valley on a trail slashing through green-needled pines, yellowing birch, and flaring maples. The path is rugged.

Neoprene chafes my skin. Sweat drips from my forehead. The trail climbs forever. Halfway to the summit, where the narrow path skirts a granite cliff, I stop to catch my breath. Dusk is falling as I bear witness to the valley and the river and the trout one last time. As I survey endless, forested hills folding towards Canada, a fleeting vision of Cynthia standing over Claire's crib interrupts my reflection. The image fades and I resume walking towards the parking lot full in the knowledge of what I must do.

Kulkuri
(Vagabond)

They call me Electric Jerry but my given name is Jorma. Like the famous guitar player, though I was born before Jorma Kaukonen was known to the world as the lead guitarist of Jefferson Airplane and Hot Tuna. Because of my age, my folks—Paavo and Rado Kantokorpi—couldn't have named me *after* Kaukonen.

I grew up in Makinen, just south of Aurora, Minnesota but not the Aurora imagined by novelist William Kent Krueger. Krueger has created a version of the town incorporating stately pines, gabbroic cliffs, and an Edenic lake. The "real" Aurora has no lake, no crags exposing the Canadian Shield, and the only evergreens found inside the city limits are ornamental cedars and yews planted in residents' yards. But while Aurora doesn't come close to the wilderness outpost Krueger conjures, it has an abundance of bars, an American Legion Post, some greasy spoons, Ed Kokotovich's barber shop, a medical clinic, a public library, clusters of bungalows and tract houses, and Mesabi East High School—known as Aurora High when I graduated in 1968.

Aurora also has dust. Or used to have dust. A thin film of gray—residue emitted by the taconite processing plant in nearby Hoyt Lakes—once defined the place. The plant is closed. Has been for years. Folks anxiously await a retrofitting of the facility to allow the processing of copper/nickel ore. Pack-Sackers from the Twin Cities have filed lawsuits blocking the proposal, claiming a re-opened plant and its affiliated mine will put the St. Louis River at risk. Thanks to the granola crowd it'll be years before the court battles are over and deserving Iron Range folks are back to work.

I didn't grow up in town. When I wasn't riding a big yellow bus to and from Aurora—getting, as my old man likes to say, "Edgeumacated"—I spent my youth exploring Makinen, a rural, woodsy, swampy part of St. Louis County settled by Finnish immigrants. My great grandfather—Salu Kantokorpi—came from Oulu, Finland to work the underground iron ore mines of the Mesabi Range in the early 20th century. After being caught up in a miners' strike, Salu found himself without a paycheck and tried to survive by farming forty acres of stumpage. Once the big timber was cut down, the logging concern had no use for the wasteland left behind, which allowed Salu to buy his forty on the cheap. Salu's wife, my great grandmother—Anna-Leena—and their two sons, one of whom (Timo) was my grandfather, joined Salu in America a few years after Salu emigrated. Grandpa Timo followed Great Grandpa Salu into the mines once suspicion towards the Finns dissipated. Timo's brother, Great Uncle Martti, didn't stick. After graduating high school, Martti shortened the family surname to "Korpi" and left Minnesota for the warmer climate, golden beaches, and beautiful girls of southern California. Family scuttlebutt is that Martti got into oil and made a killing; though since no one in the family has ever heard from Martti or his descendants, that bit of history is likely bullshit; a jealous fabrication started by those left behind to grub in the Minnesota dirt as miners and farmers.

    My sister Aada and I were born at home; in the little dovetailed-log farmhouse Great Grandfather Salu built. Like Grandpa Timo, my sister never left Makinen. Aada's been to Minneapolis to shop a few times and once Aada and her husband, Herb, drove to the Mayo Clinic in Rochester after Aada found a lump in her breast. But that's it. My younger sister, mother to a brood of six—three of each—is as rooted in the stony St. Louis County soil as our ancestors reposed in the St. Mark's Lutheran cemetery in nearby Palo. On the other hand, I escaped Makinen after "accepting" President Johnson's "invitation" to visit Vietnam.

    I spent my time with the Marine Corps in 'Nam marching, crawling, ducking, sweating, cursing, picking leeches, swatting flies and mosquitoes, drinking, and whoring. A few months before my tour was up I got shot in the foot. It's not what you think. My squad was in base camp cleaning our M-16s when a brother Marine forgot to unload his weapon. The rifle discharged and I got hit, which resulted in me winning a Purple Heart and a date with Peggy, the registered nurse who cared for me and I tried to marry, but who had the good sense to recognize something was haywire in my brain. Peggy McInnes was a red-haired beauty with milky white skin and freckles as numerous as the stars in the northern Minnesota sky. Though she said she loved me, Peggy said "no" to my proposal without so much as a second thought.

    After my honorable discharge, I headed to Alaska where I worked as a laborer. When laid off and desperate, I also worked on fishing boats plying the Bering Sea. It was in Alaska where the fortitude, or, as Grandpa Timo would say, my *sisu* served me well in bar fights and other scrapes. I stayed in and around Juneau for a few years until my old man found me a job at Erie Mining in Hoyt Lakes where he worked. I was lucky enough to snag a primo gig. I went to work driving Euclids, enormous dump trucks hauling rock from the open pit mine to the processing plant where the taconite was separated from waste rock and compressed into pellets. From Hoyt Lakes, the pellets were shipped by rail to Taconite Harbor on Lake Superior's North Shore and then loaded onto ore boats for delivery to Eastern steel mills.

Like I said, Peggy McInnes saw something in me and tried to convince me that the crippling depression I experienced in Saigon, where she tended my foot wound and I made the pitch for us to spend our lives together, was more than mere melancholia. Peggy endured nights where, after making love and basking in sex's afterglow, she tried to sleep. At two in the morning I'd pick up the six-string Martin I'd won in a poker game and abuse that guitar until dawn, convincing myself I was Jimi Hendrix reincarnated. I dismissed Peggy's diagnosis and remained oblivious to my descent into lunacy. I was hell-bent to ride my personal rollercoaster of mania and depression, hoping, as I plummeted towards despair, to arrest my free-fall by smoking pot. Peggy suggested I get help but I was too stubborn or too sick to accept her view of things. My bipolar disease remained untreated for years until, when I was back in northeastern Minnesota working for Erie and making a life for myself, that damnable illness cost me everything.

It wasn't like the disease immediately ruined my life when I came home. Before things blew apart, I fell in love with and married Sarah Jane Putilla, a tiny blonde a decade younger than me. We met when she sat next to me at a Guess Who concert in Duluth. She was elfishly pretty, with steely eyes and dimples as deep as Lake Superior, and when she noticed Joey McCarthy (a buddy from high school who also worked at Erie) and I sharing a doobie during "Running Back to Saskatoon," she wanted in. One thing led to another and soon Sarah and I were living together in a trailer behind my parents' house. With me making good money driving Eucs and Sarah working full-time as a waitress at Emil's Italian Café in Aurora, our first year together was bliss. Then Sarah got pregnant and had to quit work to be on bedrest due to complications. A few weeks later, I got laid off and the whole damn thing turned sour—like milk left out in the sun. By the time Grete Anna-Leena Kantokorpi was born we were destitute; my unemployment had run out; Dad was also on layoff from Erie and couldn't help; our car—a 1969 Chev Nova—threw a rod; and the stress of Sarah's failed attempts to breast feed, her obsession with the faint, barely discernable stretch marks marring her formerly unblemished tummy, and her post-partum funk finally broke me. I don't remember how I ended up on the fourth floor of Miller Dwan Hospital in Duluth a few days before my birthday, but I turned thirty-five in the hospital's locked psychiatric unit.

My folks sat me down in the living room of the Kantokorpi farmhouse once I got better, once a psychiatrist got me on the right meds. Sitting with my folks on their davenport, Dad explained what had happened. Or at least, Sarah's version of what had happened. I'd grabbed a twelve gauge (Grandpa Timo's Model '97 Winchester) out of the unlocked gun cabinet in my parents' garage, wandered into the trailer, and sent a couple of blasts through the bedroom door. Sarah was hiding—with Grete cradled in her arms—under our bed. I'm told I was as drunk as a skunk and high as a kite, having discovered an old stash of weed in the Nova's trunk. They say I smoked an entire dime bag on top of guzzling a twelve pack of Old Milwaukee. Mom speculates I was self-medicating, trying to best the darkness suffocating my mind. The precipitating event of my undoing? Sarah asking for money—after I'd smoked all that pot and drank all that beer—to get her hair done. She'd gone three months without a cut and color and, feeling whole again and content in motherhood, she wanted to keep things positive. She claimed my response to her innocent request was to slap her face. No dialogue. No discussion. No, "We can't afford it, Honey." Sarah's version was that I reached out and slapped her so hard she fell backwards and hit her head on an end table, opening up a nasty gash on her head. The next part, I sort of recall.

I remember yelling at her, using words a husband should never use towards his wife. Blood dribbled from my wife's head and stained the new carpeting we'd put in just before I was laid off. Grete was sitting on the couch watching it all. That's the part, more than anything else, I wish hadn't happened. I'm also sorry I lost it and hit my wife in front of our kid. No doubt about that. That slap cost me everything. When I stormed out of the house in search of a gun, my mind having lost all constraints and limitations, and my wife having locked herself and Grete in our bedroom, Sarah told my mom that was it. The slap, the look in my eyes, the bloodied head. That was, according to my ex-wife's confession to my folks, the last straw. And that was before I came back into the trailer carrying an antique shotgun, blew apart our bedroom door, and put an exclamation point on the whole shitty affair.

Now I'm living in a shed behind Hugo's Bar in Brimson, Minnesota, a few miles from where I grew up. My folks are gone. They're not dead: They retired to Arizona right around the time Sarah divorced me and rekindled something with an ex-boyfriend, a guy—Delbert Erickson—who lost his wife to pancreatic cancer. Delbert's a good man who works steady as a union electrician.

"And best of all," Sarah said to my folks when she met them in Prescott—halfway between Sarah and Del's place in Flagstaff and Mom and Dad's condo in Scottsdale—Sarah wanting Grete to see her grandparents despite me being out of the picture, "Del's real calm; no temper whatsoever," the unspoken comparison to me obvious but honest.

Grete graduated from the University of Northern Arizona and according to Mom and Dad (who are both over ninety and slowing down) is doing well. I haven't seen her since that horrific day. When Sarah and I divorced, I signed away my parental rights to Grete. That was thirty years ago. You might ask, "Jorma, what have you been doing with yourself since you nearly murdered your family?"

I take my meds. The problem is, that once the shit hit the fan and I was unable to work—drawing Social Security Disability as my only source of income beyond the handyman jobs I do for Trish and Ernie Wirtanen, the owners of Hugo's, the folks who, despite being decades younger than I am, are my legal guardians—I've found that when I'm manic, I'm a damn good guitarist. With the mania and the depression restrained by lithium—the peaks and valleys managed into predictability—my musicianship becomes commonplace. I long for the days when I played twenty hours straight, pulling songs and tunes and rhythms from my soul into the tips of my calloused fingers, reaching undiminished musical climax after climax. But the Wirtanens—Trish in particular; she works at White Community Hospital as a registered nurse—keep me grounded. Trish can detect, like a bat sensing a moth, my yearning to seek ecstasy despite a risk of perpetual gloom.

I live behind Hugo's in an old chicken coop. The main room is crowded with a single bed, a teeny refrigerator, a metal desk, an old office chair, a futon, a microwave, a hot plate, and an ancient RCA television. Then there's the bathroom: a closet-sized space that includes a shower, a utility sink, and a toilet that works only after a second flush. Hot water is supplied by an on-demand water heater. There's no medicine cabinet, no vanity. I keep my meds and toiletries in a cloth Walmart bag hanging on the doorknob. I have no internet, no telephone, no computer, no iPad, or cell phone. I *do* have wire shelves screwed into the wall behind the bathroom door where I store pans, a coffee pot, dishes, utensils, cereal boxes, packaged foods, and canned goods.

    I own a Realistic turntable, an old Marantz receiver, and a pair of long-in-tooth Advent speakers. The stereo components sit on a 2x6 pine board spanning two cement blocks. My vinyl collection is arranged in alphabetical order—by guitarist—on the floor below the shelf. From Beck to Burton to Clapton to Hendrix to Johnson to Kaukonen to King to Raitt to West to Young my collection includes the best of the best. They're my friends. They're my inspiration. They're my solace in times of tearfulness; when I think of my daughter, once a little girl, now a grown woman, who hasn't seen me in decades. If she suddenly showed up at my door, I'd likely run for cover. I wouldn't know where to begin. I nearly killed Grete and Sarah that afternoon so many years ago. It's better that Grete doesn't try to make up for lost time. I'm just not worth it.

    Friday and Saturday nights I put on a show for the regulars. Most nights, no more than a dozen folks show up to drink, play pool, eat pizza and burgers, and listen politely while I noodle on an old Telecaster. When the mood strikes, I'll reach behind my Marshall amp and pull out my LaPlante twelve-string—a locally crafted guitar I bought a few years back. I'll drag out the acoustic when things are settled and launch into a Robert Johnson or a Charlie Parr or a Leo Kottke tune. If the mood strikes me, I might toss in a little Guthrie or Springsteen or Brown or Chapin-Carpenter or Goodman or Mitchell or Dylan or Prine and sing a bit. It's during such reflective interludes I hear the whispers and rumors of an exaggerated past.

    "Ya, dat's Electric Jerry. Kilt his wife and baby girl. Plumb crazy. Got off on a 'sanity defense."

    "Heard he was in 'Nam. Heard he lost his mind after seeing a buddy blown to bits."

    "Damn, this guy's good! Too bad he spent so much time in the joint for murder ..."

    "Ya know, he grew up just down the road, on the old Kantokorpi place."

"I hear he was wounded—got the Medal of Honor—in 'Nam. Damn shame a war hero ends up playin' a dump like this."
"Ain't he Paavo's and Rado's kid?"
"Didn't he play with Jefferson Airplane at Woodstock?"
And so it goes.

Hemingway's Mistress

It started when I fell in love with his words. I was sixteen years old, a neophyte writer of indiscriminate prose when I first read *For Whom the Bell Tolls*. He was, of course, long dead—decades dead—by the time I stumbled across his body of work and started reading his stories. I'd curl up with Ernest's words on the quilt Aunt Grace made for the antique four-post bed tucked into the attic of my childhood home, the space luxurious and open and free just like I wanted to be. Only I wasn't; I was raised by conservative Catholics to be a lady. Which meant keeping my eyes lowered, my thoughts to myself, and my knees perpetually locked against sin. It was there—in my attic bedroom, constantly harangued by Christ and the saints and the martyrs and the pope and the Blessed Virgin about my purity and my eternal soul as I reposed on that goose-down quilt covering a hand-me-down bed—where I traveled to Italy and Spain and Paris and Cuba and Key West and the green hills of Africa as the voyeuristic lover of a dead man.

At sixteen, I didn't have what Ernest, beautifully formed and chiseled—you know, the Hadley and Paris version of what later devolved into a bloated, sick, alcoholic, depressive old man—had: love, in all its variants and shapes and sizes with lovers to match. I was a virgin when I began reading Hemingway, and in some ways his stories, not the early stuff—the Nick Adams vignettes—but the more adult, more sensual, more sexualized pieces, stole my innocence. I was too young to understand the lecherous misogyny behind Papa's tales. But that didn't matter to a young woman-in-formation curled in a fetal position in her childhood bed, a copy of the posthumously released *The Garden of Eden* held away from her small, brown eyes so that every word, every blessed phrase written by the Master could be lapped up like the nectar of an expectant lily slurped by a yearning hummingbird.

I imagined myself not as Catherine, the wife in the story, but Marita—the interloper into the marriage bed of the Bournes—who intimately satisfies both husband and wife. I only vaguely understood the mechanics of whatever transpired beneath the sheets. Thankfully, for the sake of art and beauty and sanctimony, Hemingway did not, as so many modern writers do, delve into the physical intricacies of lovemaking by describing the couplings in the manner of some weird biological treatise. Still, there was power behind Hemingway's innuendo that left me wondering, and—if truth be told—anxious and breathless. I did not act upon those beginning pangs of interest. I made no discoveries of self that involved sinning in the bed that once belonged to my maternal grandparents. I did not explore my still growing and maturing body in response to the tension and tenderness and sensuality depicted by Hemingway's stories. Such discovery would have to wait. But those scenes did start me wondering.

More important than opening my youthful, inexperienced eyes and heart to the possibilities of love, the old man's words—most profoundly, the scenes he painted of romance and longing and ardor and war in his greatest works, *For Whom the Bell Tolls* and *A Farewell to Arms*—taught me to write what I felt and saw and knew. His use of autobiographical material was conjured and cajoled and corrupted from *the* truth into *a* truth, like the storyline he invented concerning Catherine Barkley.

I learned, long after reading the novel for the second time, that the author's infatuation with Agnes von Kurowsky, a nurse who cared for Hemingway after he was wounded driving an ambulance on the Italian front during the Great War, was the inspiration for Catherine. But the rest? Ah, that was, as my mother used to say when reading to me from children's books, all "make believe." The affair. The child. The stillbirth. The death of the hero's beloved. It was all made up.

"So that's how it is!" I exclaimed one night after reading *Hemingway: A Life Without Consequences*, an exhaustive biography of the Great One where the secrets and tricks and chicanery behind Hemingway's metamorphic adaptations of reality into fantasy were laid bare for a young writer to see. "You take snippets of real life and then simply spin a yarn—launching a story—letting it take its own course for better or for worse."

The scenes of battle and danger and dread set against passion depicted in *For Whom the Bell Tolls* were similar sleights of hand. From Mellow's exhaustive biography I learned of Papa's torrid affair—while still married to his second wife—with Martha Gellhorn, another writer of note who, along with Hemingway, traipsed off to Spain in the late 1930s to cover the Spanish Civil War. As he'd done in *Garden of Eden*, my beloved muse portrays himself as the hero. In *Bell*, it's Robert Jordan, an American who takes up arms with the Republicans against Franco's Fascists while falling in love with a Spanish guerrilla, Maria. Hemingway himself did, on at least one occasion, actually take up arms against the Fascists but never, as depicted in *Bell*, sacrificed himself for Martha Gellhorn on the battlefield. Again, as I buried myself beneath Auntie Grace's quilt against the northern Wisconsin winter in the attic bedroom of my family's Port Wing Victorian, scribbling notes in the margins of Papa's novels, I learned storytelling and plot and character. It was also during these late night sessions that Ernest and I became lovers; lovers of pace and timing and bursts of narration that propel words across paper and into the readers mind, forever burning the gist of story into one's soul.

My English teacher at South Shore High, Mr. Warren, never understood. An effeminate man, closeted despite the rapidly changing mores of the early 21st century, Mr. Warren's taste in literature included Flaubert and Dickens and Tolstoy. His opinion of Hemingway? "Trash. Tripe. Tortured adulterous poppycock conceived in the dark recesses of a sick mind." Mr. Warren didn't mince words when it came to his abhorrence of my beloved's literary legacy!

Pointing out (as I did on several occasions) that Hemingway received not only the Pulitzer but the Nobel didn't sway Mr. Warren. I made my case in front of my classmates despite that fact that *The Old Man and the Sea* never really moved me. To me, the story, lacking sexual tension and romantic entanglement and centered upon an uninspiring human character and a doomed fish, bored me to tears. Despite my lukewarm appreciation for the novella, the fact is, *Old Man* did win the Nobel. But the reality—that Hemingway had earned the world's most prestigious literary award—did nothing to abate Mr. Warren's criticisms.

"Bah!" the thin, skeletal Ichabod-Crane-like teacher exclaimed. "Miss Johnson, you best not confuse what the masses love to read and the critics love to embrace with fine literature. That would be," Mr. Warren asserted, thumping his hand on the cover of my beloved first edition of *In Our Time* resting on my desk (a treasure my uncle Thomas found secreted in a box of stuff donated to Saint Francis Xavier for the annual church rummage sale) "a tragedy for someone as astute as you."

Bullshit, I thought, though of course, being a proper young lady from a proper family, I did not curse aloud. *Hem lived life large and open and vast, something that you, you senile old ass, have no capacity to appreciate.* But I was working on an "A" in the class: I needed the grade to get into the Main U at Madison, where, if things went right, I'd earn my master's in creative writing, a subsequent post in academia, publication of my short stories, and finally, the triumphant release of an as-yet-unwritten, acclaimed first novel. With a firm grasp on the future, I kept my mouth shut and let the old windbag dither on.

My first time, I was twenty. One would think, having been influenced and educated by Ernest in the affairs of the heart, I would've caved earlier. Oh, don't get me wrong. There were ample dates when, on a Friday night after a school dance or a football or basketball game, I found myself with Doug or Vince or Steve or whomever in the backseat of a car, the front seat occupied by my best friend, Becky Underwood, another Catholic girl but one who'd lost her virginity in eighth grade. Becky would invariably be locked in a romantic encounter with her beau of the moment, sometimes sans sweater or blouse but still wearing her bra, sometimes sans every stitch of clothing except her stockings, unconcerned about what she was displaying to the world, while I pondered the limits of teenage lust I was willing to oblige. When it finally did happen, the guy—Ben Strongitharm, an Ojibwe kid from Bad River who had a hell of a jump shot and was so damn built and cute he could be in a Guess Jeans ad—wasn't experienced or nuanced. There was no Frederick Henry artistry behind what happened. My shirt was unbuttoned. My bra was around my waist. I was reclined on the rear bench seat. Our connection involved a lot of lips meeting and tongues touching and fingers fumbling. Then, he was in, and nearly instantly, it was over. I felt nothing like the stirrings or magical feelings or passion depicted by my literary lover in his novels. Instead, I felt only extreme relief colored by a smidge of regret.

    Thing is, I wasn't on the pill like Becky. Actually, she was, if I remember it right, on birth control shots. Thankfully, despite allowing Ben to do what he needed to do that night, we didn't make a baby. Also, let's be clear; no great love story unfolded after our fondling and the culmination of ... Well, what does one call it? It wasn't lovemaking, because there was no "love" behind what we did. It wasn't, to be coarse, "fucking," because that term, to me, denotes aloofness to the whole encounter that discounts the emotions involved. "Exchange?" Boy, that sounds downright commercial; like some sort of transactional experience. Maybe I'm at a loss for the right word.

Maybe I'm no Ernest Hemingway when it comes to chronicling the vagaries of human love.

I still have all of Ernest's novels and short stories except for that copy of *In Our Time* Uncle Thomas gave me. I hadn't realized that my copy, a first edition published in London in 1925, was worth over twenty grand! When I found that out, well, as much as I love my muse, I had an education to fund: The sale of that book saw me through the master's program at UW. Maybe the fact I could part with one of Hem's precious literary gems shows I've grown wiser—less "girlish" if you will—regarding my infatuation.

    I *can* say that my relationships with men have been more adult, more satisfying as I've meandered around my twenties. I'm still not married. I have no children. But there's a guy who's marriageable, if that's what unfolds for us. For now, our bond is a pleasant diversion from the day to day of teaching undergrads how to discern good works by great authors. Maybe we'll get hitched. Maybe not. I will say this: I'll likely be better at marriage than Ernest Hemingway was.

    The real news doesn't concern my personal story. You'll read no revelations of torrid affairs here. Despite spinning towards agnosticism, I retain too much Papist discretion to kiss and tell. No, the real scoop is that my first novel, a story about a Lake Superior fisherman who risks it all to bring a doctor to his cottage on Otter Island during the Armistice Day storm of 1940, has been optioned to Scribner's. Now that's poetic justice, eh? A story about a fisherman and big water accepted by Hemingway's publisher.

The Angle:
A Novella

Chapter One

She lived in the Northwest Angle; that little protrusion of Minnesota shoving itself like a bully's thumb into Canada's eye. To get to the Angle by car, you leave the U.S. and travel through Manitoba before re-entering the northern-most portion of the Lower Forty-Eight. Alternatively, after ice-out and before freeze-up, you can travel by boat across Lake of the Woods while remaining entirely in American waters. You can also fly to the Angle through U.S. airspace. Or, if you're brave and fearless, you can—in the dead of winter—drive the tortured ice road connecting Warroad to the Angle across frozen U.S. waters but that seemingly endless trek across creaky, groaning, cracking ice is not for the faint of heart.

Adeline Susan Prettyhorse taught school at Angle Inlet Elementary. I knew her. I grew up with her. She was, despite having two children by two different fathers, someone her students looked up to; someone *I* looked up to. I fell in love with Adie when I lived in Warroad and worked for the Canadian National Railroad. I was an engineer on the run from Warroad to Koochiching County; on trains hauling wheat and barley from neighboring farms to the Koochiching cooperative grain elevator in International Falls and returning to Warroad with box cars full of lumber for Marvin Windows.

Though the Angle—part of Lake of the Woods County—contains hundreds of square miles incorporated into a single township, less than one hundred and sixty people call the place home. Most of the Angle isn't owned by white folks. Seventy percent of the Angle's land mass—including islands adjacent to the American mainland—is actually controlled by the Red Lake Band of Chippewa (Ojibwe), though precious few Indians actually live there.

Adie was one of them. She grew up on a family resort on the eastern shore of Brush Island where exposed granite and remnant white and red pine rise above the lakeshore a few hundred feet from an imaginary, watery border dividing Ontario and Minnesota. Adie's dad, Amos Prettyhorse, pure Red Lake Ojibwe, and her mom, Barbara Comstock, English and Scottish-blooded from Kenora, had four kids—Adie being the second oldest—but never married. It's been said that Barbara, despite procreating such an impressive brood, doesn't fully trust Amos, whose Indian name is *Aandeg*, which means

31

"crow," a sobriquet synonymous with cleverness. Even so, Amos and Barb have been together for over thirty years.

Adie was, like all of her siblings, born at home. Despite her patrician upbringing, Barbara was—and still is—impressively tough. Though she lived the sheltered life of a rich girl—her father being the president of the largest bank between Thunder Bay and Winnipeg and her mother being a famous essayist and literary critic whose work has appeared in all the major Canadian newspapers and whose memoir garnered the Governor General's Award—Barbara Comstock is no shrinking violet when it comes to elbow grease, hard work, and making a go of it in the bush. Pushing out four children on an island in the middle of nowhere, sixty-plus miles from the nearest hospital, wasn't a problem for the short, boyishly handsome Canadian woman who fell in love with an Ojibwe fishing guide. That connection happened when Barbara and her boyfriend-of-the-moment checked into the East Bay Resort on Brush Island in the early '70s. Adeline took after Barbara: she did not display, even as a young girl, the proclivities of her father. She was even-keeled and kindly disposed by nature, rarely arguing with her siblings and always obeying her parents, with one exception: Adie was unable to remain chaste. She lost her virginity long before I came into the picture and, for whatever reason, had decided to forgo the pill or condoms or other methods of pregnancy prevention despite constant attempts by Barbara to preclude babies being made.

Chloe was born during Adie's sophomore year at Warroad High School where Adeline was the point guard on the girls' varsity basketball team and where I was a senior closer on the baseball team. Unlike other girls who found themselves "in trouble" in Warroad due to long winters, the boredom incumbent with living in a farming community tucked into the most distant corner of Minnesota, and defiant reluctance to seek birth control from the town's only pharmacy, Adie did not conceal the burgeoning life inside her. Having conceived Chloe the summer between her freshman and sophomore years, Adie didn't miss a single game on the hard court until she was in her eighth month. Prideful and stoic, Adie ignored the jeers and catcalls from opposing fans and maintained her poise until the fetus was too large to ignore; the girth and weight and imposition of the Chloe-to-be causing Adie to lose her ability to drain three pointers sometime after New Year's. Adie had her baby in the Roseau hospital, took two weeks off from school, and then, with her infant daughter in tow, returned to Warroad High where she endured snickering and pointed fingers—from boys and girls alike—with aplomb. Her basketball coach, an understanding and counterculture lesbian, Miss Harris, made sure Adie could nurse the baby in the privacy of the coach's office between classes.

Principal Elmer Evans tried to block Adie from staying in school, citing her "immorality" as reason enough to boot her from Warroad High. When Evans attempted to banish the girl, it wasn't Barbara who forced the imperious principal's hand; it was Amos, the quietly serious fishing guide and resort owner who stepped up to the plate, marched into Evans's office with his pregnant daughter, and told the rotund administrator what was what.

"One word, Elmer," Amos Prettyhorse had said while sitting in Evans's office with his daughter. "Lawsuit."

Principal Evans looked incredulous. He wasn't stupid: He knew Amos and Barbara had means. They weren't some trailer trash who couldn't rub two nickels together, what with the success of the resort and Barb's savings and stock options gifted to her by her parents. Still, Evans couldn't believe that an Indian, one who'd never uttered so much as a "Hey" to him when they passed each other in downtown Warroad, was challenging his authority. But rather than assert his presumed power, Elmer Evans found himself intimidated by the sinewy Ojibwe with the slicked-back ebony hair and stone-cold, asphalt eyes. "How's that?"

"You heard me. You try to keep Adeline from her studies, try to send her to Roseau, to that there class for pregnant girls, separate her from her friends and her team and her coach, and I'll raise holy hell."

Evans pondered the threat. He was about to explain how the local judge, a man he went to church with in Roseau, would likely side with the school. He was also ready to praise the school district's lawyers, Twin Citians with fancy Ivy League degrees and tons of courtroom experience, who'd mop up the floor with any local yokel Amos Prettyhorse signed on with. He never got a chance.

Amos had smiled. "I know what you're thinking, Elmer. That this shabby Indian in front of you will get homered in front of Judge Clancy. That your expensive suits from Minneapolis will waltz in and make short work of any attorney I hire." Amos looked at Adie before continuing. "Thing is, my brother, Dave, you know, the head of the Red Lake Tribal Council? Well, he's got a pocketful of expensive lawyers ready to do battle. All very skilled and every bit as polished as your folks. Even so, it would be a tough fight in front of Clancy. But that's not where this thing will play out."

The principal shifted his bulk and looked at his hands. "How so?"

"We'll be suing you in federal court. In St. Paul. The school won't have the luxury of picking the judge who'll hear the case. Dave's lawyers are itching to put this thing in front of a federal judge. Something about equal protection and due process. It'll cost the school district a fortune in legal fees and, chances are, in the end, you'll be letting this young lady back into your building *and* paying damages and *our* legal fees to boot. I'd think twice about what it is you seem hell bent on doing, if I was you."

Elmer Evans had been shocked. The Indian had spoken more words in that one conversation than he'd ever heard the man utter in all their years living together in northwestern Minnesota.

Adie returned to school. Her junior year she played point guard and had a great season. There was talk of a D2 scholarship—based upon her athleticism and her grades—to Bemidji State. But one night, Adie found herself on the bench seat of Junior Benson's F150 parked on the shoreline of Lake of the Woods. No booze was involved. Adie had watched her father slowly, deliberately, and with little regret fall into insipid alcoholism as Barbara drew more and more emotionally distant from the family. As a result, Adie never touched alcohol until she was of age.

A big part of the parental rift was caused by Barbara's following in her mother's footsteps. After the arrival of Anthony—the last Prettyhorse child born two years after Adie's younger sister Joanie—Barbara had her tubes tied and started taking on-line writing courses. She found her voice and began crafting short stories that she fired off to contests. A handful of pieces were accepted for publication. Success meant not only notoriety for Barbara Comstock: It meant a book deal and, ultimately, the completion of a novel that was accepted by a Canadian publisher without Barbara hiring an agent.

Book tours and hotel rooms and travel across the United States and Canada in promotion of that first book, *Choices*—a generational story about Scottish immigrants to Thunder Bay, Ontario and the Great War—followed, taking Barbara farther and farther from home.

On the eleventh hour of the eleventh day of the eleventh month, the guns fell silent ...

Watching her father's loss of faith in his union with Barbara, sensing the pain her mother's emotional distance caused Amos as Barbara became more and more busy with her new life, and knowing the devastating impact Amos's reliance upon Molson and Jack Daniels was having upon the man, Adie had forsaken joining her schoolmates in drinking keg beer or cheap wine at pit parties or bonfires by the lake or in the dimly lighted rec rooms of friends' homes.

Timmy was conceived in Junior Benson's truck that summer night and disrupted what was supposed to be Adie's most productive season. Adie's second kid was pushed out in February, just as the Lady Warriors were on the cusp of advancing to the state tournament. The pregnant point guard was on the bench for the playoff run, so plump with child that she could barely walk much less rebound or shoot or dribble. The team missed her in the backcourt and failed to get out of regionals.

Unlike the confrontation that took place before Chloe's birth, there was no need for Amos to approach Principal Evans about Adeline staying in school. The fat man had learned his lesson. And despite Coach Sharon Harris's disappointment regarding her star player's choices ("I said I'd buy you condoms if you were gonna keep up that nonsense, Girl"), the coach's office again became Adie's nursing station and sanctuary.

Nearly two when Timmy came along, Chloe remained behind on Brush Island cared for by Amos's sister, Aunt Eleanor, who'd moved up from Thief River to run the resort on account of Barb's absence and Amos's drinking. Adie stayed in Warroad with Timmy while school was in session.

When Adie matriculated from Angle Inlet's one-room schoolhouse to middle school, she joined older brother Tom staying with Reverend Johnson and his wife—a childless couple—in Warroad from Sunday through Friday night during the school year. The arrangement, one common for families living in the Angle, meant that the Prettyhorse kids didn't have to risk blizzards or thunderstorms to travel sixty miles one way to attend school. In Adeline's sophomore year—Tom's senior year—they were joined by sister Joanie; the two girls sharing an upstairs bedroom and Tom claiming the basement of the Methodist parsonage. Mrs. Johnson was only too happy, once Timmy entered the picture, to provide daycare for the infant while Adie attended school. Timmy only spent time in Coach Harris's office if the parson's wife ran out of bottled breast milk and the child needed to nurse. Despite morning sickness, labor, birth, and the rigors of caring for two kids, Adie graduated from Warroad High with honors, a testament to her father's fortitude and her mother's brains.

Like I said, being that Warroad is a small place and we went to a small school, I became aware of the pretty sophomore Indian girl my senior year. We weren't friends. We didn't run in the same circles. We didn't date during high school. My disinterest in Adie wasn't due to the fact she had kids: I really didn't give a goddamn about that. *That's her business*, I remember thinking at the time, hearing some of the senior girls sniping and gossiping, the word "slut" prominently pronounced during whispered conversations in the school cafeteria as I ate nearly indigestible lunchroom pizza. *You prisses should just shut the fuck up,* is what I thought. At the time, I was trying to date one of the girls spouting such garbage, trying like hell not to end my senior year a virgin. I kept my mouth shut but remained "unspoiled" until I was nineteen, my silence accomplishing nothing.

It wasn't until after Adie graduated from high school that we connected and fell in love.

Chapter Two

I couldn't catch a break. I had a wicked curve but my fastball never topped eighty-two miles per hour, which meant no college recruited me to be their closer, the guy who comes in at the end of a baseball game and shuts the opposition down. I had ten saves my senior season and a respectable 2.1 earned run average. But I gave up five homers—showing college scouts I was vulnerable to power hitters—and ended up with a one win, three loss record. I was, in a word, serviceable as a high school pitcher. But college? That remained to be seen.

After mucking around minimum wage jobs in and around Warroad, I toyed with the idea of walking on at the University of Minnesota-Duluth, a D2 school, or approaching St. Scholastica, a private D3 college (also in Duluth), about a tryout. But Uncle Joe, my mom's youngest brother, told me the Canadian National (CN) was hiring, looking for conductors. I know what you're thinking. You're thinking, *A conductor: The person who takes your ticket when you get on the train.* Nope. I'm not talking about passenger trains. I'm talking about freight trains and the men and women who make sure the cars are connected and in working order and that all the signals and switches along the track are operational.

"You go through conductor's school and, in a year or two, you can apply to become an engineer," Joe said one hot, humid, August night as we sipped cold beer on the deck of the Big Lake Tavern (BLT) in Warroad. Joe was sweating up a storm. He'd just finished playing center field on our town ball team, the Warroad Wizards. We'd taken a thumping from the Green Machine from East Grand Forks. "Besides—after those two dingers you gave up," Joe said with a smirk, raising his glass to players from East Grand Forks sitting at a nearby table, "I'm pretty sure college ball isn't in your future."

In the two summers since graduation, I'd played sixty-plus games. Coach Limoseth, the honorary mayor of Island Inlet—there being no actual governance to the place beyond the Lake of the Woods County Board—had taken to starting me at second base. He rarely, if ever, called upon me to start a game as a pitcher but had no problem giving me the ball in the eighth or the ninth inning if our starter was in trouble. I was a mediocre hitter, batting eighth or ninth, my average somewhere in the mid-200s with little power, though I was a capable base runner. Truth is, in the games I pitched, I was less than stellar. My curve was serviceable, but my fastball had diminished to where a good woman's softball pitcher could match its speed. Plus, even though I still toyed with the idea of trying college ball, I never worked on a third or fourth pitch, something vitally necessary if I was serious about taking things to the next level. "You're right, Joe. I think I've hit the limit of my talent."

    Joe chortled. "Ya, well, you didn't lose the game tonight. Tubby Talbot, was godawful." My uncle paused, sipped beer from his mug, and smiled. "How the hell do you misplay two routine flies in one inning?"

    I shook my head and drained my glass of Guinness.

    "I mean, I get he's put on twenty pounds since last season. Laid off from Marvin, what with the Great Recession and all." My uncle looked at me and grinned. "Being fat has nothing to do with watching the ball into your mitt. Even you could have snagged those two."

    "Maybe." I caught the eye of a pretty young thing, a dark-haired, short, compact woman whose tan legs—muscular and tight in the khaki shorts that were part of the servers' uniform at BLT—seemed familiar. "Ma'am," I said quietly, the stout not quite yet taking hold, "another Guinness?"

    She approached and smiled, revealing jagged, irregular teeth that gleamed like small pearls. "Sure," she said without a hint of interest as she retrieved my empty and wandered off.

    "Cute kid," Joe remarked, watching the young lady sashay through the tables and chairs, every seat on the deck occupied. "Know her?"

    I stroked my chin. "One of the Prettyhorse kids from the Angle," I said with indecision. "She was a couple years behind me in school. Has a kid or two. Can't remember her first name, though."

    My uncle winked. "Kids, eh? Best stay away from her. Likely looking to get married." He paused and watched the barmaid interact with the bartender. "Still, she's a pretty little thing, ain't she?"

    My stout arrived and I made eye contact with the waitress though the only words exchanged were transactional. "We're running a tab. Eddie at the bar has my card," I said, knowing that I was close to my debit card limit, my summer job guiding walleye fishermen nearly at an end, my savings and checking accounts barely above water given my rent, car payment, and the general expenses associated with breathing.

"Got it," she said, a hint of recognition behind her enigmatic smile.

We didn't acknowledge each other more formally, and if she had been waiting for something more from me, something to hang onto and turn into conversation, that moment passed as I sat, tongue-tied, trying not to stare at her chest. The waitress walked away and I returned to Uncle Joe.

"What the hell?"

"What?"

"No ring, that's what. You could at least make small talk, see where it goes."

I sighed. "Adie," I said quietly. "Her name's Adeline Prettyhorse." I paused. "You told me to stay away from her. Make up your mind, will ya?" I paused before continuing. "The CN's hiring, you say?"

Joe nodded. "Conductors. Good money. I can get you in the door. I'm only a lowly switchman but I know people. I've got friends in HR. Let me see what I can do."

I didn't reply. My attention remained focused on the shapely Ojibwe girl standing at the bar, the declining sun still radiating heat, the sweat of the ball game and desire rolling off me like summer rain.

Chapter Three

Adie's reputation for passion had either cooled in maturity or been tempered by life. When we first started dating, not long after I began my training as a conductor with the CN, there were only fleeting goodnight kisses on the cheek and kindred hugs. No petting. No open mouths. No fondling. No romps in the front seat or the back seat of my 2002 Nissan Xterra with our shirts open to skin and our jeans clumped around our ankles. The summer we became reacquainted, Adie waitressing at the BLT and living near Warroad at her sister Joanie's place—Adie craving subtle distance from her parents but also needing to earn money for college and me swilling Guinness after home games—wasn't when we began seeing each other. It was later that year, after she'd enrolled in college and was back on Brush Island over Christmas break, that Adie and I found common ground.

 She was home from the University of Winnipeg helping Aunt Eleanor run the resort, trying to earn money for school. Adie's mom bought a two-bedroom condo in downtown Winnipeg because she was teaching creative writing at the university as an adjunct. "The pay is for shit," Barbara admitted when Adeline showed up, plastic bins of toys and children's clothes and a small suitcase of her own clothing in tow to begin her college education in Manitoba's capital, "but it pays the mortgage on this place and gives me the freedom to do what I need to do to stay sane." Barbara's real source of income was *Choices*, the novel having sold more than 50,000 copies in the States and Canada in hard cover. She was working on a second book, something to do with a rebellious Catholic priest and the Métis, the mixed-blooded people of Manitoba, and the execution of their leader, Louis Riel. Despite teaching nearly full-time and writing every morning for two hours before trundling off to teach, Barbara provided respite care for the kids in the evenings while Adie studied. During the day the children attended Sister McNamara Elementary a few blocks from the university. But when I finally connected with Adie, the kids, Chloe—six and Timmy—five, were with her, at the family resort in the Angle, home on Christmas break with their mother.

  Adeline had her eye on getting a college degree in education with the goal of becoming an elementary school teacher. She was taking advantage of Minnesota's tuition reciprocity program with Manitoba to lessen the cost. When we ran into each other at the resort, Adie's mom was in Toronto on some book gig. And Adie's dad? He was around but not much help. The few encounters I had with the man during my ice fishing trip to Brush Island were curt, short, and dismissive. It was pretty clear he viewed me and my three pals with disdain. I'm fairly certain that the proud, formerly industrious Native man thought we were nothing but a bunch of drunken mainlanders; young roustabouts who needed to stay clear of his beloved daughter, the only Prettyhorse child at the resort when we stayed there; the other kids having grown up and moved away from the Angle. Amos never said anything to my friends or me. He just sipped hot coffee in the Great Room of the lodge, glaring at us with large, almond-shaped eyes as we sat across the room telling tall tales around a roaring fire, the smell of popping maple perfuming the room, hints of Jack Daniels wafting from the old man's cup as a tell. When he was motivated, Amos would leave his chair with a grunt and wander off to do chores at his sister's or his daughter's request, saying nothing, making not even the smallest talk with the resort's guests—who were all exclusively white folks. The most ethnic of the patrons was my buddy Clarence, a guy who claimed Cherokee blood three or four generations back. But what guy from Oklahoma doesn't? Given Clarence's yellow hair and cyan eyes, I doubted his pronouncement of Native heritage. Still do.

    I was on holiday from conductor's school. As fate would have it, I was attending training at a CN yard in Winnipeg not far from where Adie was going to school. My education in railroading commenced once Uncle Joe got me hooked up with CN's HR department. I passed the piss test; I didn't do hard drugs and the weed I occasionally enjoyed wasn't an addiction. I could, and still can, take it or leave it and, on the outside chance of making nearly a hundred grand a year on the road for the CN, I had no problem telling my fellow ballplayers and pals "no" when a joint or bowl was passed around. "Gotta stay clean," I'd say with a knowing smile, a smile that told my pals I was ready to make a change in my for-shit life.

    At the first opportunity to take a breather from training, I fired up my rattletrap Xterra and headed south. When Dave Johnson suggested a long weekend in the Angle at the old Indian's resort on Brush Island, I was flat-ass busted with only a fifty in my wallet to buy gas to get me from the resort to Winnipeg.

    "That's alright, Buddy Boy," Dave said. The guy is huge: six-six and over three hundred, a washout as a pulling guard on the UND

Fighting Hawks football team after one season who'd returned to Warroad to run his dad's hardware store in the city's dwindling and patently depressing downtown. "I hit a black jack at Seven Clans," he bragged. "Two thousand bucks. More than enough to cover you."

We packed up Clarence's Suburban, a rust bucket held together by bailing wire and faith but the only vehicle big enough to haul the four of us, a trailer, and all our gear, and headed north to ice fish.

The other guy in our quartet, Eddie Boyd, is as quiet as a mouse until his second beer. Back then, he was a friend of Clarence's and not someone I usually hung out with. Reason being, after that second beer, despite Eddie being on the puny side, he usually started a ruckus. As we relaxed around the fireplace in the resort's great room, we assigned Dave the job of keeping tabs on Eddie. Which Eddie knew. Which meant there wouldn't be any trouble seeing's how Dave could crush the guy with one hand.

"Hey."

That's the best I could do when I first encountered Adeline Prettyhorse coming around a corner in the main hallway of the resort. She was wearing a tight skirt, a sweater that defined her gender, black hose, and black rattlesnake-hide cowboy boots: what I'd later come to understand was her uniform when working the small dining hall and bar just off the main lobby of the lodge.

"Hey yourself," she replied after nearly bumping into my chest with her nose. "Neil, isn't it? Neil Donnelly?"

Adie's eyes were unassailable pools of brown that appeared ebony. Her hair, which she'd worn long but in a ponytail at the Big Water, was shorn, cut nearly to her scalp, making her a dead ringer for Dolores O'Riordan, the lead singer of the Cranberries, an unattainable symbol of desirability I've loved forever. Adie paused, scrutinizing me like a rancher inspecting a steer, waiting for me to reply. "Neil, right?" she asked again, shifting her weight with impatience.

"Right. Adie, Adie Prettyhorse. Your dad owns the place ..."

She smiled broadly. "Smart boy. Up for a little fishing?"

I nodded. *Why hadn't I seen the resemblance to Dolores before?* The question lingered, unasked, as she moved past me.

"See you in the bar?"

I was tongue tied and didn't reply as I watched her saunter away, whatever thoughts I was thinking unsaid, whatever compliment I wanted to offer shut off by shyness.

The next morning, I mustered up the courage to strike up a conversation when Adie waited on me at breakfast. I was alone. The boys were sleeping in, nursing hangovers and unwilling to venture out to the ice house in twenty-five below weather; waiting to fish later on, when the day warmed. That night, once Adeline got off shift, my pals upstairs in a hotel room toasting a great afternoon of fishing with shots of Jamison, I worked up the courage to invite Adie to take a walk. I was surprised she said "yes"; or more precisely, surprised she nodded acceptance.

"I haven't seen you around since summer," she said as we walked together, dressed for the cold in winter coats, gloves, and toques. The blue wool coat she wore nearly touched the snow, offering protection against the night, making her decision to venture outside with someone she barely knew when the mercury read minus fifteen in a skirt and sheer blouse seem less foolhardy. The hem of the coat touched her cowboy boots as we walked a shoveled sidewalk, the lights of the lodge and the guest cabins glowing yellow against pristine snowbanks. "You move away or something?"

I couldn't look at her. She was too damn beautiful, too striking, for me to attempt eye contact. Instead, I mumbled a reply about being in Winnipeg for training.

That revelation seemed to brighten her. "Winnipeg? Me too! University of Winnipeg. Teaching program. You going to college up there? Using the reciprocity program?"

She conveyed information that made my heart miss a beat. *She's living in Winnipeg!* I shook my head and cleared my throat. We came to the end of the sidewalk. Beyond a neat windrow of planted red pines the frozen lake spread out towards Canada. "Got a job with the CN. Conductor." As I talked, my breath formed little clouds. I relaxed and expounded a bit on where I thought I was headed. "I want to come back to the States and work out of Warroad. Live in town. Buy a house. Become an engineer. Settle down."

She nodded but passed no judgment.

"How about you? It's a four-year program, right? Once you're done, where do you want to end up?" I stopped talking. We turned into a slight wind and kept walking. I mustered up hopefulness in my next question. "I've been watching your kids. Looks like they really love it up here. You thinking of coming back home to teach?"

Adie bit her lip. "Look," she said, pointing her mittened right hand towards the sky. A meteorite slashed overhead, its passing visible through an opening in the trees. "A shooting star!"

I couldn't tell whether she was deflecting, trying to change the subject, trying to avoid the personal, or truly interested in the cosmological visitor flashing through the moonless night. "Adie?"

She stepped onto a gravel road. I followed her lead. "Just here for a couple of weeks to help out my dad." She hesitated, as if thinking what to say but not slowing her pace. "I'll be back in school for spring term. Likely go through summer. If my classes line up right," she took a breath but never looked at me as she spoke, "I'll finish in two and a half years. That's the plan anyway."

For a short woman, she had a long stride. *Likely the result of playing so much round ball.*

"Yes," she finally admitted, returning to my observation. "My kids love being at the resort. Gives them a chance to strike off and explore; gets them out of the condo we share with my mom in the city."

We started back. Nothing else was said between us as we made our way towards the lodge. As I remember those first shared moments, it seems to me we parted with mutually uncertain nods, hesitant smiles, and nothing more. I do recall Adie opening the weathered pine door leading to the family's living quarters, hopeful that she'd glance back and say something. That didn't happen. Instead, hinges creaked, Adie slipped inside, and the door closed. I heard the "click" of a deadbolt as I walked towards the building's main entrance, my heart racing, my mind pondering whether my first, tenuous connection with Adeline Prettyhorse was worth pursuing.

Chapter Four

My upbringing in northwestern Minnesota was about as far from being raised on an island as one could imagine. When I considered making a play for the former basketball star and unwed mother of two, I found myself staring at the reality of our disparate backgrounds. She's a child of the Lake and the woods and the isolation of the Angle and I'm the son of a wheat farmer whose land once included fifteen hundred acres of the finest dirt in Roseau County. The disparate places we hail from are so different, even the grouse living in the places Adie and I call home aren't the same.

When I was ten, without worrying about the niceties of Minnesota DNR regulations, my old man, Ciarán Donnelly—the pureblooded son of Irish immigrants whose speech was so affected by his parents' lilt, folks in our neck of the woods swore that Da was "right off the boat"— handed me an old Savage side by side .410 and sent me into the swales and crannies of our farm. "They're out there, Boyo," he said with confidence. "Them sharpies are everywhere, especially in the low lyin' places. Get us a couple for Sunday dinner, would ya?"

I mean, that's how he talked, me Da. There I was, ten years old, no training beyond being shown where the safety was and how to aim down the twin barrels of that little gun. I remember going out that crisp, clear, fall day dressed in Wranglers and an old Warroad Warriors sweatshirt—a hand-me-down from my older brother, my only sibling. Mom had three miscarriages between Augie and me; Augie being ten years my senior and out of the house by the time I started hunting. I remember leaving my mom that morning (Emmy, short for Emelia, a gorgeous woman of so many ethnicities I gave up trying to remember what I was besides Irish and French Canadian) back at the farmhouse baking something, the pouch of my hoodie stuffed with shotgun shells.

We didn't eat grouse that Sunday. My dog Mike (named after Da's hero, Michael Collins)—a bouncing, youthful yellow Lab—nosed up a half-dozen birds. I shot at and missed them all. I even missed a lone straggler sitting on the branch of a skinny aspen leaning over Juniper Creek, a tiny meander crossing our land. Didn't come close to hitting that stupid bird. Despite my failure, Da was okay with me coming home empty-handed.

"You'll get 'em next time, Boyo," he said, placing his left arm around me. "Now it's time you learned how to clean a shotgun." That was Da. Infinitely patient, kind, and loving. When he keeled over from a massive widow-maker at age forty-two, leaving Mom and me alone on the farm, Augie long gone, having immigrated to Athlone—the place our paternal grandparents had run from—finding work there as a software engineer, I was the one who found Da. In the spring mud of the west field. Alongside the old International 606 he used to plant seeds with, the engine still running, his body already cooling. He'd died face up, his eyes open, staring into the vast prairie sky. I was fourteen. Mom wanted to stay on the land and make a go of it but that proved impossible. After a couple of hard years, she sold off the place and, because the farm was without debt, ended up being one of the richest women in Warroad. She used some of the proceeds from the sale to buy a nondescript two-story Cape Cod in town. Despite her bank account, Emelia Donnelly remains a modest, serene woman. Her one bow to luxury is a condo in Hawaii, her sanctuary from northwestern Minnesota's brutal winters.

"Your Da, as different as we were," she said after our move to town, "is the only man I could ever love." Mom, though warm and mothering to her sons as we grew up, could be emotionally rigid. She didn't tear up when she made this pronouncement. Oh, don't get me wrong; over the years since Da's passing, she's had boyfriends and—I'm sure—lovers, though as her son, I wished I hadn't pronounced that assumption as fact!

After spending my early years in the country, I became a town kid. Much was lost to me in that transition. I likely would've ended up in juvie—serving time for mischief—if my mother's younger brother Joe hadn't taken me under his wing and introduced me to sports.

I turned into a decent high school pitcher under Uncle Joe's tutelage. I also ended up, given my strong right arm and my harder than normal Irish head, becoming a fair quarterback and linebacker on the football team. I was built to throw, tall and lanky with little body fat. Not the build of a stereotypical middle linebacker. But I used my reach and innate fearlessness to advantage. Any success I had in sports was due to Uncle Joe, who, despite being just a kid himself (he's only three years older than me), was skilled in turning a sullen teenager's anger at God into controlled rage.

In time, though, I never forgot Da; with sports and my teammates and coaches as my therapists, I relegated the sadness and disjointedness of losing him to a distant corner of my persona. I've never fully healed from Da's sudden passing but I did escape perpetual moroseness through constant motion and by coming to a rapprochement with Catholicism and God. I'll be honest: I hated God for a while. But sometime in my late teens the Creator and I came to an accord; an unsettled, shaky understanding; a truce, as it were.

I said earlier that even the grouse are different in the places Adeline Prettyhorse and I grew up. You already know that my family's farm was inhabited by sharptail; partridge of the open fields. The Angle—where Adie hails from—isn't sharpie country. It's home to two other grouse species: ruffed grouse that favor aspen woodlands, and spruce grouse that prefer piney forests. Once I obtained my driver's license, I spent time hunting all three species of grouse inhabiting the fields and woods surrounding Lake of the Woods, though the difference in topography between where I was raised and where Adeline's family put down roots is more than a disparity in partridge.

Adie grew up knowing that if something was lacking or needed repair she had to get along without whatever it was that had been forgotten or lost or figure out a way to fix what was broken. Trips to the grocery store for food, to the department store for dry goods, to the hardware store for parts or supplies, to the dentist for a sore tooth, or to the clinic to see a doctor take a full day whether you travel by car through Manitoba or motor down the lake. If you live on the Angle, every trip to town must be orchestrated to ensure maximum coverage of any and all wants and needs.

What struck me early on as Adie and I began dating was that despite the careful nature of the Prettyhorse family's decision-making when it came to the simple, rudimentary tasks of living, Adeline didn't plan around her desire, at least until *we* became intimate. It was with me that Adie, for the first time so far as I know, insisted on her partner using birth control. Mind you, she didn't go visit her doctor and get on the pill or take the shots. She simply bought condoms from the nearest convenience store and had them handy. I know, I know. As the other half of the equation, it should've fallen on me to take precautions. I never wanted to diminish the passion, the rush of adrenalin, the spontaneity of our lovemaking by interrupting things to put on a rubber. But Adie had been through enough to appreciate the consequences of impetuousness. When it finally happened, she insisted and I complied. The rigors of living a planned, ordained existence on the farthest shores of the farthest reach of Minnesota finally came to fruition in Adeline's refusal to proceed without protection and I acquiesced. How could I not? I loved her.

It began as most contemporary affairs of the heart begin—with dinner and a movie. Adie caught a ride from Brush Island to Warroad. For our fifth or sixth date, we met up in town and ended up seeing *Revolutionary Road* with Kate Winslet and Leonardo DiCaprio at the Roso Theater in Roseau. Not the sort of flick I'd choose but I wanted to make a favorable impression. When Adie batted her big browns at me and said how she simply "adored" the two actors in *Titanic* (I have to admit, Rose *was* hot getting naked in that old car) I caved. I agreed to sit through a "relationship" film rather than take in the original *Iron Man* at the Grand in Baudette. There isn't a theater in Warroad so those were our choices; love and angst and heartache in Roseau or things blowing up and evil henchmen getting their just desserts in Baudette. I went along with Adie's preference hoping my malleability would make an impression.

    I splurged on dinner at the Brickhouse. I had the crunchy Manitoba walleye. Adie had the Cajun shrimp alfredo. We shared a bottle of Merlot. She asked, because she rarely drank, what I thought would go with shrimp. I had no freakin' idea so I just looked for something that seemed reasonably priced and sounded familiar. Like I said, and like you've probably figured out by now given my paternity, I'm partial to Guinness: I'm not a wine guy. Whatever. We ordered. We drank. We talked.

"What made you decide to become a conductor?"

She was dressed in a shimmering silk blouse—rose colored, I think—a skirt of darker red, and those omnipresent cowboy boots, their black snakeskin shining beneath the lights of the old creamery as we talked and ate. She didn't wear lipstick, at least so far as I could tell. Her face—her complexion a dusky mix of Ojibwe and the British Isles seemed natural, without makeup. Her eyelashes were long and dark and hooded her eyes. She was earnest and direct, as if she was really interested in unraveling the "why" behind me choosing to become a railroader.

"Ran out of options."

"How so?"

I smiled, picked up my wine glass, sloshed red around a bit as if I knew what I was doing, took an inordinately large sip, and nodded. "Thought I could go to college and play ball. Didn't work out."

"Whatdoyoumean?"

I sliced off a piece of fish, stabbed it with my fork, dipped it in tartar sauce, lifted it near my mouth, but hesitated so I could answer. "I wasn't all that good. Thought I was in high school. But the truth is, I only had average stuff. Fastball was nothin' special." I paused, took a bite of fish, and swallowed. "Curve ball was my 'go to' pitch. But I got lazy, didn't work at it." I looked at my date. "And then time sort of passed me by."

"I heard you were pretty good. And though I never saw you play baseball, I went to a couple of football games your senior year. You had a terrific arm."

"OK, I guess. But I was too slow thinking to do anything past high school in football. Baseball would have been my ticket if I had put any effort into developing pitches beyond my fastball and curve." I took a gulp of wine. Despite my initial nervousness at asking her out, over the course of our dates, I'd grown comfortable with Adie. "I lived and died by my curve and didn't put in the time to get any better. My Uncle Joe—you met him at the Big Water last summer—he plays on the same town ball team with me. Works for the CN. He got me in the door with the railroad when he figured I wasn't going to play college ball." As I finished answering her question about the "why" behind my going to conductor's school, I realized I'd conveyed the same information twice. *Shit. Why can't I just say things once, be done with 'em, and move on to talking about what she's up to, how her kids are, what her dreams entail?* "And what about you? I mean, where do you see yourself settling down once you're done with college?" I finally asked.

"Mrs. Ogilvie, the teacher at Angle Inlet, is retiring," Adie said quietly, wiping wine from her lips with the tip of a cloth napkin. "Given my dad's cousin Patty LeBeau is the chair of the school board, I think I have a pretty good shot at replacing Mrs. Ogilvie."

"You'd go back, live in the middle of nowhere, teaching, what, a dozen little kids living in the Angle? Sounds lonely. And a little boring."

She nodded. "True. But it's my home, you know. My kids like the isolation, the natural world, the freedom they experience when they visit the resort. I'm not much of a fisherman or hunter but I can't see myself living in town." She paused and tipped her wine glass, which she'd emptied, towards me.

I lifted the bottle of Merlot and filled her glass halfway. Someone told me that it's improper to fill a glass with wine. Why that's so, I have no earthly idea but without knowing why, I followed the admonition.

"You seem to be doing okay in Winnipeg, which is filled with people."

Adie nodded, and then did something unexpected. She placed her wine glass on the white tablecloth, reached out and touched the back of my right hand with long, narrow fingers. "True. But like you, I'm just living there, trying to better myself. I'll be back in class soon enough. Dad will have to figure out what he wants to do with the resort. My aunt is about at the end of her rope having to run the place with scant help from him. Once I'm done with school, as much as I enjoy the cultural aspects of a big city: the museums, the zoo, the food, the easy access to whatever one needs, I can't see myself anywhere but teaching in a country schoolhouse."

As we sat in the warmth of the Brickhouse, deciding who we were and where we were headed, a scene from *Revolutionary Road* manifested in my mind. I think it was the look on Adie's face, a look of curiosity, or perhaps wistful longing—I'm unable to recall it exactly—that triggered my digression.

"Have you ever been to Paris?" Frank asked April.
"I've never been anywhere."
"Maybe I'll take you with me then. I'm going back the first chance I get," Frank said. "People are alive there. Not like here. All I know, April, is I want to feel things; really feel them."

I want to feel things, Adie, really feel them ... Of course, I didn't try to replay the film in real time with my companion, a woman who I'd dated a few times, kissed once on the lips, and made small talk with. I didn't believe we were anywhere close to being boyfriend and girlfriend. There was an aloofness to Adeline that seemed impenetrable despite her fingers touching the bare skin of my hand in a restaurant.

"You're deep in thought," she noted, removing her hand, raising her glass, and sipping elegantly. "What's on your mind?"

I cast a sideways glance at Adie's quixotic face. My cheeks flamed a bit as I recalled another scene from the movie.

"I'm gonna finally figure out what I want to do," Frank said.

"*I felt that way once,*" April replied.

"When?"

"*The first time you made love to me.*"

Desire reared up. I couldn't discern whether the emotional surge I felt was due to my mind imagining a naked Kate Winslet or a naked Adeline Prettyhorse.

"Neil?" Adie's voice startled me.

"Just thinking about how this will go if you decide to move back to the Angle and I get a job in Warroad with the CN," I lied.

Adie grinned. "Remember April from the movie?"

Shit. She's read my fucking mind! I nodded.

"She said, when Frank was hesitating about Paris, 'It takes backbone to lead the life you want.'"

"Meaning?"

"I need to do what I need to do. You need to follow your vision, your quest as my Ojibwe elders would say. Otherwise, we'll end up like my folks."

Her words carried a hint of transparent warning. I thought I knew what she meant. Still, I had to ask. "So where does that leave us?"

She shook her head. Her black hair, still cropped short, barely moved. "I have no idea. All I'm saying is I don't want to end up like my parents. There was love there, once. But something changed. Maybe it was my mom exercising her independence, getting out of the house, making her way in the world." She paused and drank the last of the Merlot from her glass. I looked to add more, the bottle being nearly empty, but she shook her head. "I've had enough."

I tipped the bottle into my glass. *Two and a half glasses of wine and I'm buzzed.*

"Or maybe my dad's sadness at being left alone on Brush Island, all of his kids living their lives outside of his love and his influence. Sure, I come back to help out. My kids would die if they didn't get to see Grandpa on a regular basis. They love my old man. And when they're around, the drinking is controlled. He tries hard to stay sober when Chloe and Timmy are underfoot." There was a deep sigh. "I like you, Neil. Like you a lot. More than I've shown. But we both have to follow our own paths. I'm unsure, as we sit here, talking things through, what the hell that means for us."

There it was. Confirmation. *She likes me. Has feelings for me. Thinks of us, well, as an "us"!* It was my turn to reach out and touch Adie's forearm. Her skin was soft and warm. I left my hand in place as I replied. "No pressure. If you need to go back home and teach school where you grew up, you'll hear no complaint from me."

A frown crossed her brow but she did not remove my hand. "You'd *let* me teach at the Inlet school? How generous!" The pique in her voice was obvious.

I shook my head. "That's not what I meant." I paused, getting my thoughts in order before diving in. "I meant we both need, as your Native relatives might say, to walk our own roads. Mine is to be an engineer and live and raise a family in a town, in Warroad if possible." I stopped to consider what I'd revealed. *Funny. I grew up on a farm. Had a hard time adjusting to life in Warroad. And now, that's the only life I want.* I pulled myself out of self-reflection. "Your dream is to become a teacher, move home to watch over your dad and keep him safe." I stopped, removed my hand from her arm, and touched her left cheek. "Okay?"

It was her turn to nod.

That night, we made love for the first time. In my old bed. In my mother's bungalow on Roosevelt Street. Don't get all judgmental on me. Mom was gone, off to her condo in Kaua'i for the winter. I had a key because I was taking care of the place. Making sure the heat was on and the pipes didn't freeze. There wasn't a lot of conversation leading up to us being naked in my old bed. My intention was to take Adie back to Brush Island via the ice road. Lake of the Woods was covered with two feet of ice, plenty of support for the Xterra. There was no danger of the Nissan breaking through and the two of us either drowning or dying of hypothermia. As we drove towards the lakeshore Adie asked: "Isn't there someplace we could go—to be alone, I mean?"

The question blew me away.

"*It takes backbone to lead the life you want," April said to Frank as she talked about the life they would lead in Paris.*

"Mom's."

Adie was looking out the passenger window, seemingly lost in thought. "Really? You think I want to meet your mother, have a hot cup of tea, and talk about what a good little boy you were growing up on the farm?" She posed the question with a hint of humor.

"She's in Kaua'i. I'm watching the house for the winter."

"Ah. Then Mother's place it is!"

She was far more reserved and shyer about things under the sheets than I expected. After all, Adie did have a bit of a reputation, having procreated two kids with two different boys in high school. The kids were, in fact, with Chloe's father for the weekend. The guy was exercising his once-a-month visitation with both kids. Timmy's father, Junior Benson, got *two* weekends a month because he was more involved in Timmy's life. Junior *also* watched over both children on his weekends. Exchanges with the fathers took place halfway between Winnipeg and Warroad and required an orchestration of international law that seemed inordinately complex.

    Adie insisted I undress in the bathroom. It was clear she didn't want me watching her disrobe. By the time I returned to the room, Adie was nude beneath the flannel sheets of my adolescence, the patchwork quilt my Irish grandmother brought with her from Athlone providing warmth against a bitterly cold February night. The room was dark. I dearly wanted to see her body, to visualize unexplored nooks and crannies and curves before we touched. That didn't happen. There was no light save for the distant glow of a nightlight in the bathroom down the hall. I was unable to see details beyond a glint of light reflected in her eyes and an occasional glimpse of nipple and stomach and thigh. We kissed. Our tongues met. Fingers touched skin. There was a stiffening of resolve. I reached for the condom Adie had placed on the nightstand and put it on. Moistness of intimacy and the mutual rapidity of breathing followed. Words were said, though the word "love" wasn't uttered. It was too early in our relationship for such sentimentality. Even so, it was clear to me that something had changed. Some new understanding, affection, or recognition asserted itself and caused us to climb over the wall of fear and hesitation that begins all relationships between men and women who've loved and lost love to circumstance, cruelty, or uncertainty.

    I'd lost my virginity at nineteen. I'll not bore you with the details other than to say, I met a girl, a lonely, mournful girl at the Big Lake Tavern whom I knew from buying groceries at the local grocery store where she was a cashier. Her first name was Dolly. I don't recall her last name. It happened in the front seat of my Xterra without any thought of the consequences. It wasn't memorable. For either of us, I'm afraid. I had no idea what a woman might want from such an encounter and was ill-equipped to provide whatever it was Dolly needed. It was over, my "thanks, you're great" the last words said between us as she pulled up her panties and jeans, straightened her hair, adjusted her bra, and left me to ponder what the hell had just happened.

    After Dolly, I dated a couple of young women who taught me something about making love. Not much, mind you. Just something. When Adie and I came together in my boyhood bed, the tortured face of a nearly naked and crucified Jesus staring at us from across the room as a witness to our sin, I'm pretty sure I'd learned enough to ensure Adie fell asleep satisfied.

Chapter Five

Three months at the Winnipeg CN training facility in classrooms and working the yard, and then I was on the road. One year in service as a conductor, making the run between Warroad and I' Falls, another three months of schooling, an apprenticeship, and I'd become a railroad engineer. In short order—in less than two years—I'd be working my dream job while living in my old bedroom in Mom's bungalow on Roosevelt Street. That was the plan; to live with Emelia Donnelly, save money, and marry the girl I loved. Like a Nora Ephron screenplay, right? Didn't turn out that way. I blame God, the guy who took Da, for how things went south. Wouldn't you?

    Is it a nightmare when the terror that wakes you from deep sleep is something that's happened already? Or is there another name for such dreams? I mean, folks talk about nightmares being premonitions of a future they fear: The death of a child or a partner or a parent usually figures prominently in such nighttime episodes. But that's not what I'm talking about. What I experience is more like what soldiers deal with after surviving combat. Something dark and sinister and adhesive sticks to your soul, reminding you at the oddest times, in your lowest moments, of trauma. I'm talking about real life events; not some fantasy spun by your out-of-control unconscious mind during REM sleep. But before we talk about what's ailing me, you need to know what happened between Adie and me. I mean, that's what this story is about, right? The good times we shared: the laughs, the tenderness, the brilliant effervescence of love. That's the stuff you want to know about. Not the other. OK. I'm with you on that.

    "I'm gonna figure out what I want to do," Frank Wheeler told April as they considered their move to Paris.

    "If being crazy means living life as if it matters, then I don't care if we're completely insane," April replied.

    During our time in Winnipeg, Adeline attending university, me in school or in the CN yard working towards my certification as a railroad conductor, *Revolutionary Road* wasn't the only movie we took it. Granted, alone time was dicey, what with her schedule, my schedule, and the fact that Barbara wasn't always around. I'd arrived on the scene just as Barbara was about to launch her second novel, that Catholic-priest-in-the-midst-of-the-Métis-rebellion thing I mentioned earlier. Barbara's attention, normally fixed on the kids when she was home, was otherwise occupied with the details of final editing, cover selection, formulating a marketing plan, and trying to keep Amos from burning down the family resort.

The old man was on his own. Aunt Eleanor had given up trying to manage the resort. She'd left Brush Island convinced that Amos Prettyhorse was drinking himself to death. Though Barbara fretted about Amos's imbibing and the possible conflagration of the Prettyhorses's largest investment due to carelessness or stupor, she did precious little—beyond worrying—to ensure the resort wasn't rendered a shambles.

But the point I'm making isn't about Amos or Barbara or the resort; it's that, as Adie and I continued to see each other, we took in other films, plays, local bands, and the like whenever we could find a sitter for Chloe and Timmy or whenever the kids' fathers had them for the weekend. That said, *Revolutionary Road*—maybe because it was the first flick we saw together or maybe because I'm smitten with Kate Winslet—remained *our* movie. I'm still fond of that film even if it invokes feelings of sadness and loss.

"That was nice," Adie said after the first time I went down on her. "I've never done that before."

We were in Barbara's condo, the kids away for the weekend with Chloe's father, naked as jaybirds beneath the sheets of Adie's queen-sized bed, a vintage black-and-white movie playing on an old vacuum tube TV across the room. The flickering light of the television was the only source of illumination as we sat, backs against the headrest, pillows propping up behind us, sharing a bowl of peanut M&M's.

"Blue?" When did they start to put blue ones in M&M's?"

I smiled, picked out a blue candy, tossed it in the air, and caught it in my mouth. "For like the last decade. Don't you pay attention to anything important?" I teased.

Adie's breasts—so modest that gravity had little effect on them, the nipples erect and alert in the room's chill—rested on the white cotton top sheet. I tried not to look. I tried to concentrate on the movie—an old western—but found myself making furtive glances at the girl I loved. I was still wet down there. I'd stripped off the rubber but some of my seed remained behind as a reminder of passion.

"Me neither."

Adie cocked her head, fixed her eyes on me, and crinkled her forehead. "How's that?"

My off-hand reply was in reference to her first comment and had nothing to do with the color of candy. I could see my remark puzzled Adie. I pulled the quilt to my chest. It was cold in Adie's bedroom. She liked to sleep with the thermostat set at sixty. Outside, the night was rainy and gray and blustery. Details of the slumbering city couldn't be seen through the rain-streaked windows, but I knew Winnipeg's maples were losing their leaves and that the leaves, despite being sodden from rain, were being blown about in the storm. "What we did. It was a first for me, too," I said.

Adie snuggled, pulled the quilt up to cover her chest, and rested her head against my right shoulder. I noticed that my nipples, which remained exposed, were the same size as Adie's, an anomaly that puzzled me. *I wonder what hers look like when she's pregnant? Or nursing?*

"Really? Well, you seem very proficient at it ..."

It's called the internet, Adie. You can learn all sorts of things on those websites. Again, I didn't ruin the mood by being crass. "Ya, well. I hope it was alright for you." That last part was stupid of me to say. She'd trembled like she was riding out an earthquake when things came to an end. But curiously, unlike most times we'd made love, she hadn't closed her eyes at the ultimate moment. Despite the waves of what surely must have been pleasure (or—if she was a better actress than I knew—the result of a great performance) Adeline Prettyhorse, her long black hair splayed across the pillow (she'd let it grow out again), her back arched to receive my tongue, had watched me as I tried my damnedest to make her happy. It wasn't creepy or unnerving, the way she focused on me. Her interest in what was happening caused me to concentrate, to ensure I didn't mess up. I guess, in the end, it all worked out.

The next morning, she cooked a big breakfast of hash browns and French toast and scrambled eggs and bacon. American-style bacon. Thin and fatty. Not that thick Canadian stuff. As we sat at her mother's kitchen table, mugs of hot coffee steaming, tumblers of orange juice standing sentry beside plates heaped with food, she asked questions about my training. I asked her about her kids and college. Things were solid and kind and easy; until I reminded her that my time in Winnipeg was coming to an end.

"What the hell, Neil?" There was injury in her voice. "Can't you take a job up here? I mean it's the same fucking railroad as the one you want to work for in the States."

I shook my head. "Opening's for a conductor in Warroad. That's where I can get a job. There's nothing up here for me and besides, as an American, it's one thing to come to Canada for training; it's quite another to seek residency and stay for a job."

"How's this gonna work?" she asked, upset clear in the question. "You're moving two and a half hours away? What am I? Just another piece of ass to you?"

It was our first real fight and it came out of nowhere. *Christ. We make love, have a nice time, eat a great breakfast. And then this!* I was tongue-tied and didn't really have an answer. Or, I did, but she wasn't going to like what came out of my mouth.

"Well? Answer me, Mister Railroader."

I stood up, walked around the table, and leaned over. She seemed so small, so much frailer and more vulnerable than when we were making love. Her legs had been strong. Her eyes had been clear and defiant. But now, looking at Adie wearing my far-too-big Killer Vees T-shirt as pajamas, her bare left foot tapping nervously against the linoleum floor, her strength seemed to vanish, seemed to evaporate like a rain puddle confronted by midday sun. "Don't," is all I managed to say, stroking her hair as it cascaded onto her shoulders. "Don't."

"Fuck off."

There it was. The spirit, the fire, the anger she'd exhibited on the basketball court. During games, with the crowd cheering her on, she'd been in utter and complete control of the outcome. Here, as I looked pleadingly into her eyes, tears welling and spilling down her angular cheeks, the Ojibwe in her plain and open and obvious despite her mother's ancestry, it was clear she had no game plan, no strategy for what was to come.

Chapter Six

You know from what I've revealed that things worked out between Adie and me until that godforsaken night. More about what happened later on. Now, you want to know how it was we became a long distance couple. I took that conductor's job with the CN in Warroad and moved in with Mom. I bought myself a Brittany to keep me company when my shift work with the railroad and my training as an engineer wouldn't let me visit Adeline and the kids. I named the dog Leala, which is French, Old French, I think, meaning "faithful" or "loyal." But you want to know about us, not about some damn dog.

    We came up with a routine. I couldn't expect the mother of two to drive two and a half hours in a battered old blue Mazda B4000 two-wheel drive Cab Plus pickup to Warroad. The Mazda had 120,000 tough miles on it and was long in tooth. Sure, my own Xterra had seen better days. It was getting towards the end of a pretty good run. But at least my Nissan had four-wheel drive. Adie's piece-of-crap Mazda, really no more than a glorified Ford Ranger, was useless in winter. I tried to get Adie to ask her mom for a loan so she could upgrade, even suggesting, against my better judgment, she think about getting a Subaru. But Adeline Prettyhorse was too proud to impose further on her mom. It was enough she was, in her words, "leeching off" Barbara by staying in Barbara's Winnipeg condo and having Barbara watch the kids so Adie could make classes and do her homework. Still, that old Mazda truck bothered me a lot. Turns out, I was right to be concerned.

    Other than when we first got together and made love in my old boyhood bed on Roosevelt Street, all the time we spent together, up until Adie graduated (in less than three years, I'm proud to say!) and came back to the Angle to take Mrs. Ogilvie's position at the one-room school house in Angle Inlet, was at Barbara's condo in Winnipeg. I got to know Adie's mom when I'd drive up from Warroad to spend time with Adie. Barbara was okay with a railroader dating her daughter, making it clear that since Adeline was an adult and a mother and going to school to better herself, Barbara would refrain from judging my love for her daughter. As long as we were respectful of Barbara's writing time, time she spent in the extra room of the condo next to Adie's room, Barbara was copasetic with me staying overnight. Somewhere along the line, Barbara also took Adeline aside and gave her a talking to, the result of which was that Adeline began taking birth control pills. Meaning no more condoms. I liked that, never having been fond of the things in the first place. That change didn't increase the frequency of our lovemaking or our ardor or our passion. It just made such occasions, when the kids were gone with their fathers and Barbara was off doing writerly business, more spontaneous. For the duration of Adie's time in school, we worked things through and were exclusive to each other, bonded in love, except for my one misstep.

"What the fuck, Neil?"

It happened a year and a half into our relationship, near the end of Adie's second year at the University of Winnipeg. My buddy Dave Johnson and I drove to Fargo to see Wilco at the Fargo Dome. Tickets were sky-high but, since I was working as an engineer, having put in my time as a conductor, completed the classes, done my apprenticeship, and passed all my testing, I was making more money than I'd ever thought possible. All my friends were stuck at Marvin Windows or working in local shops or stores or on family farms making peanuts or laid off and looking for work. Thanks to Uncle Joe, I'd snared the best job available in northwestern Minnesota for someone without a college degree. When Dave suggested we drive down to see Tweedy and the boys and spend the weekend in Fargo, I was all in and offered to pay for the tickets and the hotel as long as Dave drove.

We ended up pretty drunk and tuned up on some of the best weed I'd ever had. My next run to I' Falls was a week away, making me unconcerned about being piss tested. There were these two NDSU college girls. Blondes. Nicely built and giddy as hell, standing next to Dave in the front row on the main floor of the arena during the concert. One thing led to another and, without really thinking it through, we invited the girls back to our hotel. We had a few drinks in the hotel bar and got all hot and bothered but it didn't go any further. Why didn't I take that college chick up to our room? I'll tell it to you plain and simple: As I was kissing Marcy (I have no idea what her last name is), our tongues probing in desperation, my hands exploring a stranger's skin, Adeline's face manifested in my head despite the booze and the weed and the hormones. I cut it off, leaving Marcy confused, and Dave—whose hands had been all over the other blonde's ass—thoroughly pissed. Dave came back to our room a few minutes later fuming and cussing me out. I knew I'd let Dave down, though the next morning, he said he understood: "You pulled the plug because you're in love with that Indian chick."

"Adie," I said, as we sat in the café at McNally Robinson Bookstore in Grant Park, my girlfriend staring into her cup of black tea as I tried to explain, "nothing happened."

She looked up at me, her eyes teary yet firm with anger. "Then why the hell did you think I needed to know what you and that fucking Dave did after the concert?" She glared at me, which caused me to stare into my hot chocolate, hoping against hope that somehow, I could unsay what I'd said.

I don't know why I decided to tell her anything. I mean, like I said, beyond a kiss and maybe—okay that's a lie: There was some fondling and groping involved. But it was all above the waist and came to an abrupt halt. I swear. Of course, I knew very well why I opened my mouth: I was uncomfortable keeping such a thing to myself. Here we were, the kids off in the children's section of the bookstore looking for one book each—books I'd promised to pay for—with Grandma Barbara. Never Barb. Even with Chloe and Timmy she insisted on her full first name being used. You can see I'm deflecting here, trying to avoid the telling of something that was hurtful to Adie and painful to me. Simply put, I couldn't countenance holding it back, keeping a secret. Da never did that with Mom. He was the sort of man who made sure all his cards were on the table. He gave me that, the short time I had him. "All you have, Boyo, is your reputation, your good name," Da said more than once. "You screw that up, you've got nothing." So I told. After we ordered, after the kids and Barbara wandered off in search of a new Seuss or picture book, the ceiling of the place soaring above us, the warm air of summer cooled by air conditioning, the hubbub of book lovers and serious people a constant din surrounding my revelation, I told.

"Answer me, Neil." The insistence in Adie's voice was replicated in her frown and the disgust in her eyes. "If nothing happened, why the fuck did you tell me about it?"

Before I could reply, she dove deeper into that wasteland of a morning.

"I mean, was she pretty? Was she, as Dave is so fond of saying, 'fuckable'? Did you want to screw her in the bed of your hotel room? With Dave doing the same thing in the bed next to yours?"

I took a deep breath and was ready to defend myself but Adie would have none of it.

"You know what? I don't need you to answer that. You wanted to fuck her. Right? I mean, why else would you be buying her drinks, kissing her, making moves on her? What else is left, once you've crossed that line other than screwing her brains out in some rented bed far from the woman you claim to love?" Adeline stood up, tossed a crumpled paper napkin on the table before placing both hands on the tabletop for balance. "You know what? You can take a cab back to the condo. Your bag will be waiting for you at the door. Have a nice drive back to Warroad, asshole."

See what I mean? I should never have been honest and told. But I didn't want to be Frank in *Revolutionary Road.* There's that scene where he reveals he's slept with a co-worker. Perplexingly, instead of being pissed off, April isn't taken aback. Instead of yelling and screaming at Frank, April critiques human nature: *"No one forgets the truth, Frank. They just get better at lying."* I'm not good at lying and didn't want to start with Adie. I unveiled my secret and when I did, when I spilled my guts that morning in the bookstore, Adie walked away; my ability to plead my case destroyed by her clarity and her truth.

It's obvious that the scene in the bookstore wasn't the end of us. Barbara stopped at my mom's place. It was early on a Tuesday morning a month or so after the shit hit the fan. It was still summer. Heat was omnipresent despite the hour of the day when Barbara showed up unannounced and rang the doorbell of Mom's bungalow. Barbara was dressed in a cotton skirt and loose-fitting cotton blouse, nylons, and pumps looking every bit the author on her way to a bookstore signing. Which she was. She was doing *two* signings in Duluth; one at the Bookstore at Fitger's and one at Zenith Bookstore. Her second novel, *Defiance,* that story about the priest and the Métis, had just hit the shelves in hardcover. I guess the thing was selling like hotcakes. I really don't know. I'm the typical male: I rarely read books but when I do, I don't read fiction. History or biography is about it. I hadn't read Barbara's debut, *Choices,* despite Adie giving me a signed, personalized copy our first Christmas together. Just don't seem to have the time or the gumption to invest in wading into a four hundred and fifty page story about folks who don't exist who are confronted by events that never happened.

"You're being an asshole," Barbara said, her hot tea—her morning drink of choice even in swelter—sending steam towards an open window, my mom refusing to install air conditioning despite an ample savings account and growing investments.

Mom smiled. She'd heard my version of the rift and, quite frankly, given how fond she was of Adeline— "Best choice you ever made outside of listening to Uncle Joe about the CN," she'd said many a time—she was one hundred percent in agreement with Barbara as to me being a fuck-up. Of course, Mom would never use *that* word. Not even when I told her about Da lying dead in the west field. But I know she's capable of thinking it. Especially given my lapse of judgment in sucking a stranger's tongue in a hotel bar. I didn't share that tidbit with Mom but, given her experience with love and relationships, I'm pretty sure both Mom and Barbara had an inkling of what took place even though I spared them the sordid details. "Yes, Neil. Barbara's right. You're an asshole."

What was I supposed to say? *I should've never listened to Dave when he suggested we ask the girls back to the hotel. Stop it. Dave didn't make you do <u>anything</u>. It's all on you, Boyo.* The fact that Da's Irish lilt delivered that admonition inside my head threw me for a loop. *Goddamn it Da,* I thought. *Get off it, would you? I feel bad enough as it is. I don't need your criticism to make me realize the error of my ways!*

I held my tongue and listened as the women analyzed my failings. It went on and on and on. The situation seemed hopeless. My despair increased as each count of their agreed-upon indictment unfolded, was argued, and proven.

Barbara finished her tea and looked at me with fixed, hazel eyes.

Not at all like Adie's, I thought, attempting to deflect her scrutiny.

"She's willing to begin anew. Slowly, you understand? Back to square one. No sleepovers; just casual dating." Barbara reached across the kitchen table and surprisingly, for a woman of such cool aloofness, touched my cheek with a perfumed hand. "You'll need to work at winning back her trust, Neil. That is, if you still care for her."

My mother nodded. "He's smitten with your daughter, Barbara. And the kids. I also think, though he hasn't used the word with me, Neil's fully and completely in love with Adeline." Mom turned her head and stared at me. "Tell me I'm wrong, Son."

I shook my head. Tears welled. There I was, a six-foot-two, one hundred and eighty-five pound railroader, crying at my mother's table. *Shit this hurts!*

"Of course it hurts," Barbara said quietly, removing her hand from my face. "You breach a trust with someone you love, you pay the price. Pain is part of that price."

She can fucking read minds!

"So what's Neil got to do, here, Barbara, to make things right?"

Barbara stood up and smiled. "Call her."

I wiped tears away with a sleeve of my sweatshirt. "She's got my number blocked."

Barbara smiled. "Not after I leave here. I'll make sure she takes your call. Go slow, Neil. Give her time. You two are good together. It <u>will</u> work out."

My mother joined in. "Adie's the best thing to ever happen to either of my boys. I just wish my older son, Augustus, could find a nice Irish girl in Athlone and settle down. He's almost forty. A bit old to start a family." Mom paused and cast her harsh, blue eyes in my direction. "Maybe this one can be an example for his older brother."

Chapter Seven

"So this is your young man," the old woman said, eyeballing me.

"Yes. This is the railroader that Adie's become so fond of," Barbara replied, her long, thin, blue-veined hands placed carefully on the white linen table cloth of the table Adie, Barbara, Barbara's mother—Sigourney Comstock—and I occupied in the upscale dining room of the Fort Garry Hotel in downtown Winnipeg. We were only a few blocks from Barbara's condo having what Adie called a "get acquainted lunch" with her maternal grandmother. Barbara sat next to Adeline and directly across from Sigourney as a buffer against the old woman's vitriol. I was seated between Adie and her grandmother trying like hell to remain calm despite the tension in the room.

"Oh. A railroader. How *nice*."

The inflection in Mrs. Comstock's voice was condescending. Her English heritage—lineage she held onto fast and firm as a societal anchor against the influx of immigrants of dark skin and dubious faiths to her beloved Canada—was draped across Sigourney like medieval chain mail. It was clear from her refusal to look in my direction that the old woman thought little of me. No, that's not right: She thought nothing of me. In the hour I spent nibbling my pork cutlet and tossed salad and twice-baked potatoes, I don't recall Sigourney Comstock addressing me or engaging me in direct conversation. It was as if I wasn't there.

"Yes, Grandmother," Adeline said. "He's finished school. He went to work first as a conductor, and now he's training to become an engineer with the CN."

"You mean the fellow who drives the train, don't you dear?" Sigourney corrected. "Not like a *degreed, college educated engineer* but a driver of locomotives?"

I took a deep breath. "That's right. I went straight from high school to the CN," I said, taking the pressure off of Adie. "College wasn't for me."

"I *see*," Mrs. Comstock said, avoiding my gaze even though we were seated next to each other.

Sigourney's curtness begged Barbara's intervention. It was clear, from dealing with her mother's disgust regarding the thirty years Barbara had "lived in sin" with Amos, the incessant familial turmoil exacerbated by Barbara's chosen beau being "of color," that mother and daughter had stumbled upon familiar rhetorical ground. "But there was a time, wasn't there, Neil, when you considered college? You wanted to play baseball? Right?"

I smiled weakly. "True. But I was never all that good. Plus I wasn't much of a student. In the end, I had to do something; had to get myself out of a rut. My Uncle Joe put in a good word for me with the CN."

Adie touched the back of my right wrist. "He's making really good money, Gram. Engineers are well paid."

Mrs. Comstock sipped chicken noodle soup—the only food she'd ordered—off a pewter soupspoon and didn't reply. Instead, perhaps because—to a woman of prominence and means, discussions of money are considered crass or because my biography bored the shit out of Sigourney Comstock—the old woman changed the subject. "And how is teaching in that little schoolhouse going, Dear?" she asked Adie.

Adeline had finished her coursework and her teaching practicum. After our dust up, she and I reconstituted our courtship. Over time, she renewed her faith in me and allowed me back into her children's lives. Not as a father figure: Both fathers were in the picture and doing fine jobs—despite Chloe and Timmy having been born out of wedlock—at mentoring the kids. I was cast in this play of an extended, non-traditional family as a surrogate, adoring uncle. The role fit me.

Mrs. Comstock's question called to mind the fact that Adie had finished her schooling, taken over Mrs. Ogilvie's classroom at the Angle Inlet School, and settled into the life of a teacher. She'd rented a down-on-its-luck, three bedroom mobile home from my old baseball coach, Doug Limoseth, the honorary mayor of the town and the proprietor of the only mobile home park for a hundred miles. We kept up our weekend relationship by me visiting Adie in the Angle whenever I wasn't working. I'd replaced the XTerra with a brand new, fresh-off-the-showroom floor Dodge Ram four-by-four crew cab pickup; a vehicle with enough space for two car seats, the unspoken premise of the truck being that eventually, I'd ask Adie's old man for her hand. That was coming. It was just around the bend. But it wasn't something I was going to discuss with Mrs. Comstock. No way in hell was I going to risk her ire and condemnation by revealing my intentions towards her beloved, college-educated granddaughter.

"I'm loving it, Gram."

Sigourney pushed her half-empty bowl of soup away. "Too salty. Not the best chicken noodle I've ever had," she complained. I got the sense that this was a common scene: Mrs. Comstock going to the nicest eateries in Winnipeg and whining about the food. She was, very simply, the sort of person who is perpetually unsatisfied. With food and with her only child. But with her granddaughter? Despite Adie's missteps in high school and the obvious social transgression of procreating children before marriage, the old woman displayed a mildly judgmental, patrician's forgiveness for her maverick grandchild. The other three grandchildren? I'm sure she set aside modest, cool affection for Amos's and Barbara's other kids. I was never in her presence when Adie's siblings were around so I'm only guessing here. But it was plain to me, during my initial interaction with the matriarch of the Comstock family that Sigourney held Adie in some esteem.

Barbara winced. "But this is your favorite restaurant, Mom."

"*Mother.*"

Barbara nodded in contrition. "Yes. I'd forgotten. *Mother.*"

Sigourney smiled, displaying perfectly fitted dentures. "And why do you love teaching in that dreary, drab little schoolhouse away from everything else, Dear One?"

Tenderness. She's capable of it. But it seems Adie is the sole target of her sentimentality. Doesn't appear there's anything similar available to Barbara. Likely due to Sigourney's only child, the heir to her literary talent, bedding down with and making babies with an Indian. I bet that blew the old girl's mind!

Adie smiled, placed her fork on her empty plate, and touched her right index finger to her lower lip as if in deep thought. I knew the answer to Sigourney's question and instinctively understood Adeline's gesture to be theater. She was simply taking her time, appearing to be mulling over the inquiry as if she was a witness pondering a prosecutor's question.

"Well, Grandmother, it's like this. First, the Angle Inlet schoolhouse isn't dreary or drab. Far from it. We've been blessed with modern technology; computers and internet access have opened up my students' opportunities for learning. The entire world of knowledge is at their fingertips. Plus, the school board, after closing the place down for a few years, has seen the light and invested money to upgrade the building. It's delightfully quaint." Adie kept her voice even, yet firm. She wasn't lecturing her grandmother or bluntly correcting the old woman's misconceptions. She was merely ensuring Sigourney Comstock knew where her granddaughter stood. Adie took a breath, tipped her glass of ice water to her mouth, sipped ladylike, and continued. "Plus, as you well know, the Angle is my home. It's where Mother and Father raised us. I've spent time in Warroad, which is alright for a small town, and Winnipeg, which has its attractions, I'll grant you. But living as you and Mom do, in a city, why that just isn't for me. Teaching a dozen eager kids of disparate ages in a rural schoolhouse is my dream job and I was lucky enough to land it right off the bat!"

"I *see*."

Sigourney's brusque reply was the first crack in the affection she'd shown towards Adeline. To be honest, I didn't catch the negative inflection but Barbara sure did.

"Mother. It's Adie's choice. It's Adie's life. Leave well enough alone."

The tempest came.

"Oh, so *that's* how it is!" Mrs. Comstock said, discretely intensifying her annoyance. She stared, the look hard-edged and filled with disgust, at her only child. "Here we sit, a railroader who has affection for and some unspoken hold over my granddaughter; a bright—no, more correctly, I daresay — a *brilliant* young woman with brains enough to become anything she wants. A doctor. A barrister. A professor. Or maybe, with a little mentoring, an author; and my daughter ...," the old woman stopped to exchange her wrath for something slightly less untoward before casting a pitying gaze at Barbara, "... a middle aged, mid-list novelist with four children scattered to the four winds trapped in a loveless relationship with a drunk." Sigourney paused again to gather her breath. "So you see, Daughter, where my concern regarding Adeline's lifestyle and career choices originates. I mean, really, *Barbara*. Teaching school to a dozen or so ragamuffins in the bush while trying to feed, and clothe, and care for two young children, all the while being courted by this ..." Here she stopped and established a deep-daggered condemnation of me before continuing, "... *blue-collar worker*? I should have thought, after the disaster of your living in sin with that drunken *fishing guide*, you'd be hard at work mentoring Adeline to prevent such nonsense from being perpetuated."

There it was. I'd been charged, tried, and convicted by the family matriarch. Sigourney's verdict, after one meal with me, was that

I lacked redemptive qualities. Without saying the word, Mrs. Comstock had deemed me *worthless*.

Adie glared, picked up her glass, and in one swift and unforeseen motion, tossed cold water and ice cubes into her grandmother's impenetrably pale, plastic-surgeon-enhanced face.

Adeline's reaction to her grandmother's cruelty convinced me it was time to buy the girl a ring.

Chapter Eight

Chance. Luck. Providence. Happenstance. They all have to do with the unplanned, unplotted, unscripted future each human being faces. Not that I thought I was granted an exception from life's vagaries. That sort of belief in destiny is reserved for those who are cock-sure of their place in the world. Me? When Da died, any such rock-solid faith in an orderly, perfectly configured future died with him. The absence of a father—and Mom's sorrow at losing her best friend—didn't cripple me, didn't leave me unable to get out of bed or put one foot ahead of the other, though Da's sudden demise took the wind out of my sails. His passing, the lack of his presence during my teens, is likely one reason that, while I had *some* athletic ability—perhaps enough so that I *could* have played college ball by adding additional pitches to my tool kit—I didn't make the effort.

    I have the body of a pitcher; long and thin with a whip-like right arm. But I never possessed the gumption to better myself. After Da died, standing pat was good enough. Sports got me through a rough patch but they weren't something I cared to stake my future on. Or, rather than blaming Da's passing for my blasé attitude, maybe I'm just a lazy sonofabitch. Maybe that's it: I *chose* not to go to college, not to pursue Uncle Joe's dream of me pitching at the next level. Joe was disappointed but, given he loves me, he let it slide once I followed his advice and signed on with the CN. Both he and Mom shifted their expectations for me when I took to railroading. I'm not sure I did; take to railroading, I mean. I think I was just doing what was easiest. Except when it came to Adie. There, I worked hard to make our relationship flourish. With Adeline, I knew chance and luck and providence and happenstance were not enough. I couldn't bear it after Fargo when she shut me out. I learned my lesson. I never strayed again.

        It was the coldest winter northwestern Minnesota had seen in years. We were forced to endure day after day of below-zero cold. The polar vortex that stalled over Lake of the Woods made attempting anything outside a heated building, including getting in and out of an idling locomotive, miserable. The steel grab bar adjacent to the engine's entry steps would, if you didn't remember your gloves, adhere to the bare flesh of your palm, ripping skin off your hand as you climbed. I never had that happen because I never forgot my gloves. Another engineer, a guy greener than me, did. His right hand was bandaged for a week. He was taken out of service—not because of the bandage—but because he needed Lortab to deal with the pain. Opioids and operating a two hundred ton diesel powered GE locomotive don't mix and, if you're piss tested and caught doing such a stupid thing, it's your job. The guy stayed home until the pain cleared and he was off meds. The point of me telling you this is that I never made the mistake of trying to climb into the cab of a diesel locomotive without gloves in twenty-below weather. I may not be college educated but I'm not an idiot.

I had an errand to run. My quest required me to drive to Winnipeg with the mercury stuck at fifteen below. I planned on seeing Adie and the kids on the way back but that wasn't my primary reason for driving north. Barbara and I had a date; a date at City Jewelers in the Portage Place Shopping Center in downtown Winnipeg to buy an engagement ring and a wedding band.

"Thanks for doing this, Barbara."

Like I said before it's always "Barbara." Adie's mom didn't countenance or answer to "Barb." Though she isn't as rigid as first impressions imply (she possesses a hell of a lot more compassion and depth than her mother) there's still an air of money about the woman. Privilege—and propriety—cloak Barbara Comstock like expensive fragrances. Adie didn't inherit any of that from her mother or grandmother. Adeline was, likely due to the two kids she birthed before age twenty and the tough route she'd taken to get her teaching gig, softened, rather than hardened, towards folks because of her experiences. Still, I have to give Barbara credit. Despite being a well-known author and the daughter of a wealthy banker and a famous essayist, Adie's mom was able to shed most of the pomposity and regalia Sigourney Comstock bequeathed her. In the end, while it took a bit, I grew pretty damn fond of Barbara. And I think she came to like me, all things considered.

"My pleasure, Neil."

Even though Barbara dodged some of the aspects of privilege and wealth that came with being a Comstock, when we met up in the cavernous lobby of Winnipeg's only downtown shopping center, she was dressed as if ready for a photo shoot for the book jacket of a new novel. Her hair was perfectly trimmed—the blonde color, given her age, likely artificial but perfectly matched to her alabaster skin and her gray eyes. She carried a red wool coat over her left arm and was dressed in a calf length dress of matching red, black nylons, and black pumps. But the focal point of it all was a string of natural pearls strung on gold wire resting against her milky breastbone. The necklace immediately drew one's eye to her elegantly thin, though not frail, and thoroughly feminine form. Barbara is a looker, even into middle age. It's easy to see where Adie gets her beauty from.

"I have no idea what to look for in jewelry. If you hadn't agreed to help pick out rings, I'd likely choose something Adeline would nod fake approval at and say, 'Oh, that's nice,' to conceal her true feelings."

Barbara smiled, pecked me on my right cheek, grabbed my arm, and started walking me through the mall. "Diamonds, Neil. All a girl wants or needs in an engagement ring are diamonds."

"Diamonds? Plural?" I gulped and felt anxiety rise inside me. *I've only got three grand set aside for this,* I thought. *How many diamonds and what sort of setting can you buy for three grand?* I began to suspect that I should have invited Mom to be my jewelry consultant. Though well-off in her own right due to the smart investments she made after the sale of the farm, Emelia Donnelly is no fool when it comes to money. Frugal, but not cheap. *Perhaps*, I mulled, *Mom would have been a better choice than a well-to-do novelist with blue-blooded ancestry.*

"Not to worry. What's your budget, young man?"

As she'd done during earlier conversations, my future mother-in-law had read my mind. Or maybe, with my face flushing and my heart pounding, she'd simply recognized obvious signs of distress. In any event, her question was spot on.

"Three thousand."

We arrived at the store and stopped at the threshold. "More than adequate for Adeline. If we were talking about Joanie," she said confidently, looking up and directly into my eyes with steady understanding, mentioning her youngest daughter, "you'd be a bit short. That girl shares her Grandmother Sigourney's penchant for acquiring nice things even if she can't afford them. But Adie," Barbara released her grip on the sleeve of my jacket and lowered her gaze, "is practical. She'll be happy with a three thousand dollar ring and matching band provided they're artistically pleasing."

I nodded. We entered the store. I bought rings.

On my drive to the States, I considered my timing. *There's still Amos to deal with,* I thought as the Dodge purred south along Highway 12 towards the border. The cold didn't affect the truck. Inside the cab, Neil Young's *Harvest Moon* played over the Bose sound system. I sang along—badly, since I'm nearly tone deaf—as I thought about Adie's dad. *Should I call ahead before running up to Brush Island, driving across the ice road from the Inlet, and stopping in to pay Amos a visit?*

Amos had, according to Adie and Barbara, deteriorated to the point where the resort was closed; a circumstance tremendously disappointing to the Twin Citians, Fargoites, and Chicagoans who loved the place. Many of those saddened by the closure of Prettyhorses's East Bay Resort were on their third generation of family staying at the resort. I'd only met Amos the one time, when my buddies and I were up for a weekend of ice fishing; the weekend Adie and I first connected. Amos Prettyhorse hadn't thought much of me then and I dare say, the mere fact I was employed and could provide a good life for his eldest daughter wasn't likely to change his opinion. Still, it had to be done. *What the hell. It's only three. I can be at the resort by six. Why put it off? It's not going to get any easier and Amos surely won't be any more sober or understanding a week from now. Plus this way, I can stop at Adie's, spend the night, and in the morning, ask her to marry me.*

A timber wolf, thin, old, raggedy and in need of a meal, emerged from a tamarack swamp, trotted into the left ditch, and stopped. The animal appeared to be considering whether to risk crossing the road. "Easy, old fella'," I said, slowing the Dodge, my identification of the wolf's gender a guess. "Git on across, if that's what you're thinkin'," I whispered, Neil Young's whiny voice drifting across the hot atmosphere of the Dodge's cab. The wolf didn't budge. It stood atop crusty snow, its yellow eyes squinting, studying my truck as if to say, *No thanks, pal, I'll stay over here for now.* The wolf remained planted in the ditch, its shaggy appearance a testament to hardship as I pushed against the accelerator with my right foot.

I took a chance and headed for Brush Island. Driving on ice isn't the risk I'm talking about here. I'm born and raised in that country, remember? There was more than three feet of ice as the heavy Dodge crossed the frozen surface of Lake of the Woods. I felt no trepidation related to driving across ice. My fear was related to my errand and that fact I hadn't called ahead. *Nothing says I have to ask*

for Adeline's hand from her father, I rationalized as I drove onto the island. *I could just turn around, head back to Adie's trailer, hang out for the night, and in the morning, when Chloe and Timmy are eating their hot oatmeal or scrambled eggs at the kitchen table, I could ask Adie to marry me.* But that approach smacked of cowardice.
"What the hell do you want?"
I was lucky. Amos hadn't started in on his whiskey when I knocked on the door leading to the resort's living quarters, the lodge's main entrance locked and bearing a "Closed" sign. I'm not saying Adie's dad was sober. He'd been tippling Molson since breakfast. Sipping beer was, according to Adie, her dad's way of avoiding a brutal hangover.
"He's drinking a pint of Jack every night," Adie had told me when the subject came up a few weeks before my trip to the jewelry store. "It's like he's trying to kill himself in the slowest, ugliest way possible." Adie stopped, gathered her thoughts to forestall useless tears over her father's decline, and continued. "He has four children who love him and ten grandchildren who worship him. It's not too late for Amos Prettyhorse. But it's getting there."
Given Adie's revelations I expected worse than what I saw standing in the dim light of the doorway, cold descending over Lake of the Woods as the mercury touched thirty-five below. I was dressed for winter. Toque. Insulated gloves. Sorrels. Brown insulated Carhartt jacket—its hood pulled up and over my toque. I've lived my whole life with cold. I know how to get by. Amos stood in front of me—light from the living quarters reflecting off his oily black hair, his deep brown eyes scrutinizing the *gichi-mookomaan* interrupting his peace and quiet—in a clean black T-shirt commemorating the 2007 Winnipeg Folk Festival, plaid pajama pants, and sandals. He wasn't wearing socks.
"Can I come in for a minute or two?" I asked.
"Why?"
"It's important, Amos, I wouldn't be up here pounding on your door after dark if it wasn't."
Adie's father was a head shorter than me. He'd once been as thin as a rail, sinewy and firm like a red cedar, but his stomach had expanded into a drunkard's paunch. His eyes revealed the onset of jaundice. Despite showing signs of decline, his attitude, his inner resolve, was undiminished. There was a calm, steady defiance to the man that I'd seen replicated in the woman I loved. I fully expected him to slam the door in my face. Instead, he stepped aside and

grunted: "One minute. I'll give you one minute to say whatever it is you came to say."

I stepped inside. Amos closed the thick, white pine door behind me.

"You know who I am, right?"

Amos looked up into my face and nodded. "The Irishman who's sleeping with my daughter."

Shit. This is going to take more than a minute. "We met once before. I was up here, fishing with friends a few winters ago."

"I remember."

"You're right, about your daughter I mean. Except you need to know; we're in love."

He shook his head. "Bah."

I waited for more from Amos Prettyhorse. But he said nothing. "We've been dating for a while now. I love her deeply." The words, when uttered to the father of my beloved, came out twisted and awkward.

Silence.

I dug into the pocket of my Carhartt jacket, pulled out the box from the jewelry store, opened it, and displayed the modest engagement ring and wedding band Barbara and I had settled on. The overhead light was replicated in the three white, Canadian-mined diamonds on the engagement ring. The quarter carat stone placed in the center of the white gold setting was flanked by two one-eighth carat stones; one for each of Adie's kids. "I came to ask your permission to marry Adeline," I said, my voice catching.

Amos's scrutinized the rings before focusing on me with disdain. "Okay. "

His reply puzzled me. *Was he saying, "Okay, you've done what you came to do, you've asked; now leave. Or was he voicing acquiescence?* I stood there, the jeweler's box open, the diamonds reflecting shards of light against drywall, winter's cold seeping into the room from beneath the door's weather stripping as we gauged each other.

"You asked. I answered. It's time for you to leave." Amos Prettyhorse didn't seem unduly upset with me as he opened the door and pointed to my truck idling in the gravel parking lot. I sensed that the old man's severity towards me had diminished by a small measure.

"But ..."

Amos shook his head and again pointed at the Dodge. "I said it's time for you to go. You can tell my daughter it wouldn't kill her to bring my grandchildren by for a visit. Beyond that, I have nothing more to say."

I returned the jeweler's box to a pocket of my jacket, pulled on my gloves, exited the foyer, and stepped outside. Amos slammed the door behind me; an expression of finality that echoed across frigid wilderness. I took a cleansing breath, shook my head, and walked towards the Dodge; a nearly full, omnipresent moon illuminating my retreat.

Chapter Nine

Adeline said yes.

The next morning, over oatmeal and toast, with Chloe and Timmy wearing matching Sponge Bob Square Pants pajamas, I pulled the jeweler's box from the pocket of my sweatpants. Having come prepared to stay the night, I brought my Duluth Pack rucksack with a change of underwear, clean socks, my ditty bag, a clean T-shirt, sweats, and the rings. I opened the box in front of Adie and did the "down on one knee thing" right there on the linoleum floor of the kitchen, extending the box and the rings towards Adie as she sipped hot tea.

"You know what this means, Neil?" she asked.

Once she'd accepted my proposal and I'd slipped the engagement ring on (it would need to be re-sized: both Barbara and I over-estimated the thickness of Adie's ring finger), the matching wedding band remaining in the box for future presentation, I stood up, hugged the woman I loved, and felt tears—hers and mine—wet my face. I created distance, wiped my cheeks with a paper napkin, picked up my coffee mug, and took a swig before answering. "That I need to save money for a wedding?"

Adie laughed and shook her head. "We can talk about that later. No, I was just thinking back to the first night we made love."

Oh shit. When was that again?

She caught the expression on my face and grinned impishly. "It's not a test."

I gathered my wits and thought back to how we'd started out. "*Revolutionary Road*. In Roseau. Dinner in Warroad. At the Brickhouse. And then, back to Mom's place."

She tightened the fabric belt of her terry cloth bathrobe, stood up, and kissed me on the lips, a trace of yesterday's perfume scenting her skin. "Very good, Mr. Donnelly." She sat down and gestured for me to do the same. "I've always thought that the best line in the whole picture, as sad and depressing as it was—given what happened to April—was her saying to Frank: 'We were never destined to be great or special.'"

Adeline's reference puzzled me. *Is she diminishing what we have, where we're headed?*

Like her mother, Adie instinctively understood what was going on inside my noggin. "No, silly. I'm not saying getting married will diminish *us* or *our* future. Quite the opposite. I was trying to contrast what happened to April and Frank as a couple and what's happening here."

"Oh."

The kids picked up their empty bowls and, as dutifully trained by Adie, rinsed them in the sink before placing them in the dishwater. "Can we watch Netflix?" Chloe asked, her piercingly familiar black eyes—her paternal grandfather's eyes—fixed on Adie as Timmy, less duskily complected, less outwardly Native American than his sister but still brown eyed and black haired, scampered off to the living room to turn on the flat screen I'd bought the kids for Christmas.

"One hour. It's gonna warm up and be above zero. I thought we could drive to town for lunch, do some grocery shopping, and then visit Zippel Bay later to ski the Candlelight Trail. There's gonna be a full moon. The park has a guided nighttime ski that sounds delightful. Would that work out, Neil? I mean, staying at Emelia's place, maybe going to church in the morning? The kids and I haven't been to church in ages."

The subject of religion rarely came up between us. I hadn't thought through what sort of wedding Adie would be comfortable with. I was Catholic by birthright; both me and Augie having been brought into the faith as part of our Irish heritage, Da being full-blooded, Mom being a host of ethnicities but one-quarter French Canadian. Adie had been raised Anglican by Barbara, Amos having no affinity for organized religion. But with the nearest Episcopal church being an hour and a half away from the resort, church attendance by Barbara and her brood had been sporadic. Adeline had been baptized but she'd never been confirmed and, once she left high school and went about raising her kids and attending college, other than when she lived in Winnipeg—where she managed intermittent Sunday visits to Holy Trinity Anglican with her mom and Chloe and Timmy—Adie didn't have the time or the gumption for church. When she asked to go to Sunday morning service after spending the night at Mom's place, it threw me a bit.

"Ah ..." I stammered, trying to remember the name of the little Episcopal church in Warroad. "St. Peter's?"

"Yup. Service is at ten so we'll have plenty of time to eat breakfast and get ready." She sipped tea and focused those lovely, lazy black eyes—the lids lowered in perpetuity, an aspect that rendered her gaze suggestive even when talking about God—on me. "I mean, if that's alright with you. I know you were raised Catholic and crossing the threshold into a Protestant church might be conflicting." She was teasing me, a wicked smile expanding across her small face.

"No, no. It's okay. Not a problem. I haven't been to mass in a year; something Mom reminds me of whenever she makes it to church, which isn't as often as it was when Augie and I were kids." I stopped, stroked my chin, and finished the thought. "St. Peter's will be fine."

With my build you'd think I'm a cross-country skier. Nope. My winter sport of choice is snowmobiling. I've always bought American, always Arctic Cat sleds. In fact, as Adie was suggesting a moonlight ski at Zippel Bay, I was thinking *Why not bring the kids snowmobiling instead? She can take Timmy on the older sled. I can take Chloe on the new Cat.* But I knew skiing was something Adie wanted to do as a family outing; actually, our first family outing as an engaged couple. "Okay. Moonlight skiing and church it is," I said, trying to mask my disappointment.

"You have something else you want to do?" Her voice wasn't hard-edged—just perceptive.

I shook my head.

"You've got skis, right?"

I did. An ancient pair of waxable skis with old style bindings, the kind where you insert steel pegs on the soles of your boots into holes in a steel plate. I hadn't used the skis in years. But the boots still fit. *What the hell. It might be fun.*

It was. Julianne Ramos—a Hispanic immigrant to northwest Minnesota working for the DNR—served as our unofficial guide. We hit the trail under a full moon that was more impressive than an ordinary full moon. It was a *blue* moon—the second full moon of the month—that illumed the silent, undulating terrain abutting the big lake. The oversized moon was undisturbed by clouds and cast elongated, spectral shadows of pines and birches and aspens across the narrow trail. The kids were troupers. There were no complaints from the munchkins; no pleas to pee in the woods, no whining for snacks, and no requests to cut our visit short. It was, I was certain, a portending of the lovely life we would live together as a family. Turns out I was wrong about that. Tragically, wrong.

Chapter Ten

After we ate Campbell's canned tomato soup and grilled cheese sandwiches—the only meal I'm capable of cooking without completely screwing things up—and the kids were tucked into Emelia's bed, my mom off to her Hawaiian condo with her "friend" of the moment, Adie and I made love again in my childhood bed. The familiarity of the room matched the familiarity of the act. It was pleasing beyond belief, I think, for both of us, despite the ghosts my old room contains. The one thing I was grateful for, as I stared at the ceiling, Adie snoring contentedly beside me, her face turned to the wall, her black hair tickling my left arm, was that Da's presence doesn't permeate the house.

Da never lived there so his spirit has no reason to inhabit Mom's bungalow on Roosevelt. Oh, I see him, talk to him, and visit with him—figuratively, of course—when I'm in places that mean something to Da; the fields, the woods, or on Lake of the Woods chasing walleye. Fishing is where we talk the most. Da loved a good day on the water. Is it crazy to say that I continue to learn from Da, accepting his counsel from the beyond, years after he left us? I don't think so. I mean, I'm pretty sure anyone who has suffered the sudden, unexpected loss of a parent—or any loved one—soldiers on with the expectation that they can pick up the phone and speak to the dead. I know, when things happen to me and around me, I often get the urge to call Da and get his advice. I know that's silly. There are no iPhones in heaven: Steve Jobs's reach doesn't go quite that far! But you get what I'm trying to say, right? Holding conversations in a sixteen-foot Lund on Lake of the Woods with my deceased father isn't evidence of insanity. Or is it?

The engagement really didn't change anything between Adie and me. She kept teaching in the Angle and I stayed in Warroad, working for the CN, making the run back and forth to I' Falls.

The tracks I worked run out of the Warroad switching yard and follow Highway 11 south. Here and there, gravel roads and paved highways intersect the CN right-of-way; requiring cross arms and lights at major crossings or, in the case of rural roads and driveways leading to farms and homes, simple cross bucks—white X's with the words "Railroad Crossing" painted in black lettering. As of 2009, yield or stop signs are also required by law at those places where cross bucks are in place. But the cost of inventorying all the crossings where tracks and roadways meet falls upon the railroads as does buying and installing the required signage. If I've learned anything working for the CN it's this: Railroads are slow to change. It takes time to implement new regulations. When Adie and I became engaged, not every CN crossing had been marked in compliance with federal law. Such dereliction of duty wasn't illegal: Knowing the slow, methodical approach of railroads, Congress gave the industry until 2019 to attain compliance with the new signage requirements.

    I was taught to be on the lookout for drivers who didn't observe the flashing lights that are a precursor to mechanical arms descending at automated railroad crossings. Such caution is essentially meaningless once a fully-loaded train, pulled by one or more locomotives (the number of locomotives being dependent upon the number of cars) hits speed—somewhere between fifty and sixty miles an hour. Even if an engineer *perceives* an idiot attempting to cross the tracks as the cross arms come down, there's not a lot an engineer can do in the face of such stupidity. It takes a mile and a half to stop a fully loaded train after dynamiting the brakes. At automated crossings, vehicle drivers receive ample warning: Before the cross arms descend, warning lights and bells activate and the engineer sounds the locomotive's whistle alerting drivers that a train is approaching. Fools who want to test the stopping ability of a speeding train can ignore such warnings but do so at their own peril.

    It's a far different situation at crossings where the only notices to drivers are inert cross bucks and yield or stop signs. Folks coming upon unautomated crossings receive no additional *visible* warning of danger if a train is approaching. There are no flashing lights or mechanical arms to protect against collisions. Trains *are* still required to blow their whistle before coming into the crossing but that's sort of inadequate if there's noise in the car—like a couple arguing or heavy metal music playing or an infant carrying on. It's up to vehicle drivers to be alert, listen for train whistles, look both ways, use common sense, and of course, yield to any train barreling down the tracks.

    Few drivers or passengers in vehicles survive collisions with trains. Words I used before would be appropriate here: Luck, chance, or happenstance *might* allow folks in a car or truck hit by a train to wake up in the hospital, or, more improbably, walk away from catastrophe. But that's not the usual outcome. What was instilled in me at the CN training site in Winnipeg and during my "over the tracks" apprenticeships (both as conductor and engineer) is that occupants of vehicles improvidently driven into the path of moving trains rarely survive. I was vigilant on my runs between Warroad and I' Falls; constantly searching the roads and driveways leading to unautomated crossings to ensure no one was playing the fool. I never counted on bad luck rendering my diligence impotent.

"When will you be back?"

Adie asked the question as I shaved over the bathroom sink in her trailer. Steam obscured the mirror so I wiped the glass with the edge of a towel, which did little good. I was under the gun in terms of time, rushing to get to work while trying to avoid nicking myself with the razor. The exhaust fan was on the fritz so I'd opened the window to vent the claustrophobic space but my attempts to clear the mirror weren't working.

"I'm on for the next three days. After that, I've got two days off. I'll be back on Tuesday."

"So I play the single woman for the weekend?"

"'Fraid so."

Adeline was standing behind me, fully dressed, ready for a day of teaching. Her kids were in the kitchen, eating cereal, waiting for Adie to drive them to school. We never really talked about what it's like to teach your own children. I'd made the assumption I guess, knowing her personality, her diligence to task, her near obsessive/compulsive need to attain perfection, that she was likely harder on Chloe and Timmy than her other students. But we'd never broached the topic and I wasn't about to enter precarious terrain as I tried to get ready for work.

"Church was nice."

Adie's languorous, somnolent eyes inventoried me. "Uh huh."

I wiped shaving cream from the razor with a towel, tucked the razor and can of Barbasol into my ditty bag, closed the zipper, and turned towards my fiancée. Her expression, one I'd seen a thousand times, evinced she was deep in contemplation. "Yes?"

"I was just thinking about the wedding."

"Oh?"

She leaned against the doorframe, blocking my retreat. "What would you think about a church wedding?"

I picked up my ditty bag, bent down, kissed Adeline on the left cheek, and nodded. "Not a problem. Where?"

"St. Peter's. I love that little church and my mother would be so pleased, not to mention that Grandmother might even show if we have an Episcopal service."

I sniggered. The response was unintentional but, in my mind, justified. "You mean the great writer and widow of one of northwestern Ontario's leading financial lights would deign attend the wedding of a granddaughter who tossed water and ice cubes in her face?"

Adie's cheeks reddened. But whatever I said to irk her was soon forgiven. "She'll come around. She's a stuffy old witch, Sigourney Comstock is. And not very nice at times. But she still loves me. She has to. I'm her favorite grandchild. She'll show. Mark my words."

With no basis to object to Adie's faith in her grandmother, I nodded.

"Good. It's settled. St. Peter's it is. What do you think about a fall wedding, say mid-October? The leaves will be in full color. God, it will be so beautiful!" She was gushing now, the excitement of planning the big event overtook her natural caution and made her speech quick and vibrant. "Would that be alright? I don't want to force things."

I moved Adie aside and exited the bathroom. "October is fine," I said with some emotion although I wasn't as excited about the wedding as Adie was. Don't get me wrong: I was head over heels in love with Adeline Sigourney Prettyhorse and was looking forward to marrying her. Having kids with her. Making a life with her and her two children. But beyond buying the rings and proposing, I hadn't thought through the details of a wedding, a reception, or a honeymoon—if we could swing one with our schedules. Despite my lack of forethought, I tried to convey enthusiasm. "We can talk more later. I need to get a move on. If I'm late and lose my job, our wedding reception will be held at McDonald's!"

She tittered and let me pass. "I'll see you next week," Adie said in a dreamy voice, her bedroom voice. "I might be in town when you get off. Text me. I'm supposed to take Joanie's kids for the day while she applies for jobs. Doug says it's time for her to go back to work."

The reference was to Adie's younger sister and her dipshit husband, Doug Anderson. The guy had some balls telling his young wife and the mother of two kids under five to find work when he'd been fired from Marvin Windows for showing up high on meth for the night shift. Doug had fought his dismissal, arguing no one had piss tested him. He'd won his unemployment claim; an administrative law judge finding there was no proof, beyond a supervisor's suspicion, that Doug Anderson was high while operating a fork lift. That victory just meant Doug was entitled to six months of unemployment benefits. Because Marvin is non-union and Doug's employment was at the pleasure of the company, his firing stuck. He got his twenty-six weeks of unemployment but wasn't reinstated. And Dipshit Doug (my nickname for him, which I never used in his or Joanie's presence) didn't see fit, once his benefits ran out, to make any *real* attempt to find a job; meaning his family existed on food stamps and general assistance and handouts from Amos and Barbara while he pretended to look for work. I really shouldn't have said anything in response to Adie's comment but I couldn't resist.

"Nice brother-in-law you've got there, Adeline. Real peach, making his wife go to work while he sits on the couch in his Zubaz watching porn."

My fiancée blew air between her lips so hard they flapped. "I know. He's a dipshit. I get that. But she's my only sister and asking for help. Aunt Eleanor is trying to straighten out the mess Dad's made of the resort and isn't available. My brothers live too far away. That leaves me to help out Joanie in a pinch. I'll call Mrs. Ogilvie. She's on the sub list and won't mind spending a day at her old school teaching kids. Text me Tuesday morning when you come in from the Falls."

I laced up my work boots, threw on my winter jacket, hit the remote starter on the Dodge, put on my toque and gloves, and opened the trailer's front door. A wall of cold—the mercury again below zero, the wind fierce—hit my face like a sucker punch. "I will," I said. "I love you," I added as an afterthought, not knowing what my perfunctory endearment would mean come Tuesday morning.

Chapter Eleven

Ice. It's a hazard of living in the north woods in these days of global warming.

I have to stop here before I tell the rest and make something perfectly clear. I'm apolitical: I no longer vote. I did once, back when Obama first ran. I thought it would be nice, my first time in the voting booth, to cast my ballot for a black guy. Some might cringe at my choice of words here, "nice" having the possible connotation of some sort of privilege, some aspect of me—a white working class man—thinking he was proving he's not racist by voting for a black man from Chicago. Okay. I'll give you that. The word "nice" is insipid and weak and doesn't really answer the question "why." Here's the thing: I was tired of paying for wars that seemed then—more so now—pointless and never-ending. As much as I admired the late Senator McCain for his public service, I viewed him to be a continuation of the intractable conflicts we seemed to be mired in. So Obama it was. After one visit to the voting booth, I never cared again. The optimism America felt going into 2009, or at least was felt by folks like me who voted blue, quickly dissipated in the face of the intransient Turtle Man telling his caucus: "I'm going to do everything I can to make Obama a one-term president," as if my vote and the vote of sixty-nine million other Americans didn't mean a goddamn thing. Still, I'll give the old tortoise his due: He made good on that promise. Other than the Affordable Care Act, saving the auto industry, and a few minor "wins," President Obama never really moved his agenda—an agenda I supported—ahead. Consequently, I gave up. When Romney ran in 2012 and essentially said everyone who supported Obama was a slacker (remember that secret tape?) his improvident disclosure in front of his fat-cat friends just proved my point. Politics is a waste of a working man's or woman's time. Trump didn't change that. Hillary wouldn't have changed that. No one will ever, in my view, change that.

I bring this up because, well, Adie; she didn't agree with me. Once our respective feelings about politics and elections were out in the open. we avoided those topics. I knew from our earliest conversations that Adeline was extremely liberal—maybe even a socialist—and viewed the right to vote, especially given her Ojibwe heritage, as sacred. She's the one who called the original discriminatory tone of our constitution—where indigenous people were considered members and citizens of their tribes but not citizens of the United States—to my attention. Adie argued vigorously that, given most Indians weren't considered U.S. citizens until 1924, failing to vote in <u>any</u> election — local, state, or federal—was akin to what I, a Catholic, would understand to be a mortal sin. Beyond these discussions as to *why* it was necessary for Adie to vote and be counted, we pretty much left politics alone. It's a good thing she didn't live to see Trump elected. That would, I'm certain, have changed things. Big time. She could not have avoided berating me if my apathy helped put the crown on Trump's head.

    This is a long-winded way to tell you that, while I'm apolitical, I believe that human activity, including the belching of diesel smoke from the very locomotives I once operated, is contributing to messing up the Earth's climate. How and to what extent, I'll leave to smarter minds. But I know this to be true: Winters up north have changed such that the possibility of rain in December and January and February and the resulting ice on roadways is the new reality.

    I was on my way back from I' Falls with a load of pine lumber bound for Marvin Windows. It was the Tuesday after our moonlight ski. It was early morning—or late in the evening depending upon your perspective, 5:30 a.m.—when I checked the digital clock tucked amongst the gauges in the locomotive's cab. The train was headed west on the mainline from I' Falls to Warroad. I wasn't thinking about Adie: I was thinking about sleep. I was tired and, truth be told, felt a bit under the weather after playing poker with a bunch of guys from the Kooch yard. I'd lost my shirt and thought tippling would change my luck. I know, I know. I was breaking rules, ignoring statutes, flaunting the law. If I have <u>any</u> measurable alcohol in my bloodstream when I'm on the job, I'm in violation of Rule G, the federal zero tolerance regulation for railroaders. The poker game was over by four the previous afternoon; I'd eaten a big steak dinner and slept a solid seven hours before taking charge of the train. Other than being tired, I felt fine. But blood alcohol is a curious thing. Short of taking a PBT before getting into the cab to determine whether I had alcohol in my system, I had no idea—as I operated the diesel—whether I was violating federal law or not.

    As the locomotive chugged west through the bleakness of that miserable February night, no moon shining, the stars obscured by clouds; clouds that were—despite the thermometer hanging at thirty degrees above zero—spitting rain, I felt OK. I was aware enough to perceive that the adjacent highway was slippery. I *saw* ice forming from my seat behind the controls of the locomotive. A person in a car or truck wouldn't have the advantage of looking down on the roadway from height like I did. *It's godawful out,* I remember thinking. But no one appeared to be out and about, and I felt confident that, as the big diesel chugged along at a steady fifty-two miles per hour, the run to Warroad would be uneventful.

    The conductor—Johnny Duggan—sat quietly in the cab watching the shadowed landscape roll by. We weren't friends. We didn't normally work the same crew. I don't want to imply we weren't cordial towards each other: We got along fine. But, having no real shared history, Johnny filling in for my regular conductor, Buddy Swenson—a talkative, curiously funny Swede who'd come down with mono—Duggan and I simply did our jobs and stayed out of each other's way.

    The train was nearing Williams, a half-hour east of Warroad when the rain turned to hail, a fact made obvious by the racket the pellets made bombarding the locomotive's roof. The noise of ice hitting steel would've made it difficult to hear each other if we'd been conversing, which we weren't. The storm also made it difficult to see. I knew, from countless runs to and from I' Falls, that there was a slight bend in the tracks ahead; a curve bisected by a driveway, a familiar driveway that led to an old farm owned by Doug and Joan Anderson—Adie's sister's place. I also knew that the gravel road leading to and from the Anderson farm (a misnomer since Doug didn't have the gumption to work the land or care for livestock) leaves Highway 11 at a wicked angle, and that the gravel access road climbs from the highway towards the house. Which means that traffic *leaving* the Anderson place travels downhill towards the CN tracks. On prior trips, I'd never seen any vehicles entering or leaving the Anderson Farm. I wasn't thinking about a car or truck negotiating an icy descent as my train approached the crossing.

    When the locomotive came around the bend, its headlamp picked up a vehicle that appeared to be stopped on the Andersons' side of the crossing. The train hadn't yet hit the whistle board—a signboard erected to remind engineers to sound the whistle before entering the crossing. As I kept an eye on the truck, the racket from hail striking the roof of the locomotive's cab intensified.

    "That's fucking loud," Johnny Duggan said, cupping his hands over his ears. "You see the truck?" he asked, pointing forward.

"I do."
"Looks like it's stopped."
The whistle board drew nigh. I activated the locomotive's high-pitched warning as I strained to see out the windshield. "Fuck!"
"What?"
Despite the wind-whipped hail and the darkness, I was certain of what loomed ahead: The blue truck had not stopped short of the cross buck and stop sign; it was stuck—rear wheels spinning and unable to attain traction, the empty bed of the pickup sliding back and forth— smack dab in the middle of the crossing.
I cut power to the drive wheels and jammed on the brakes. We were less than a mile from the crossing when I recognized the pickup and the profile of the driver franticly shifting from drive to reverse and back to drive in a desperate effort to move the blue Mazda out of danger.
Adie!

Chapter Twelve

Athlone has been remarkably dry. Since I walk to work each morning, rising from my narrow bed in the back bedroom of the second floor of my brother Augie's row house on Parnell Square to hoof it to Shannon River Plastics, a manufacturing facility on the west bank of the Shannon River next to Route 446 in downtown Athlone, the fair weather has been a blessing. Augie, and his live-in, Aibreann ("April"), and their new baby, Caitlyn, share the other bedroom. The newborn is a tiny thing; just six pounds a full two months after Aibreann pushed her into the world after a very difficult labor at St. Vincent's Hospital. Caitlyn was named by her mother after a favorite poet's wife. Not the wife of Yeats or Joyce or some other Irish bard. Aibreann's muse—in terms of verse—was not Irish but Welsh. I'm talking about Dylan Thomas. Caitlyn Thomas, though she had Irish ancestry (her grandfather Henry McNamara owned a large estate in County Clare and her father Frances once owned and ran The Falls Hotel in Ennistymon) was born and raised in England. That lineage created, at least in this American's mind, a puzzlement as to why an Irish lass would select the name of an Englishwoman as her daughter's namesake. I've learned such contradictions are what attracted my staid, serious brother to Aibreann. Augie loves the woman's mercurial nature. She's so very different, with her flaming red hair and green eyes, easy laugh, engaging manners, and diminutive build from my tall, dark haired, brown eyed, stuffy older brother; the contrast, if she wasn't so endearing, would be alarming.

    I knocked around a bit after quitting the CN before I agreed to visit Augie. I'd been to Ireland once before with Da and Mom and Augie on a family vacation to celebrate my brother's graduation from Michigan Tech (where Augie earned a degree in chemical engineering). After that vacation Augie decided to immigrate to Ireland on a Skilled Worker's Employment Permit. He eventually met Ireland's eight-year residency requirement for naturalization and becoming a dual citizen of Ireland and the U.S. Even though Augustus and I had never been all that close—given our disparate ages and the fact he's been living in Ireland for more than a decade—when I felt I needed a change, a drastic alteration of my life course or I'd end up dead, he greeted my telephone call with what, for such a reserved man, can only be described as muted joy.

"Brother," he had said calmly, with just the hint of support and love behind the word, "Mom told me what happened. I am so sorry."

I worked hard to avoid breaking down, sobbing like a child, as I relived the accident in my head. "Thanks."

"I'll not ask you how things are," Augie continued, refusing to allow silence, the onset of which would've likely caused me additional upset. He filled our conversation with words as distraction. "I can only imagine how you've been feeling. Mom says you are done with railroading. Is that true?"

"Ya."

"So you're not working?"

"Not since the accident—except for some laboring jobs and working as a fishing guide. Just enough for gas money, insurance, and to pay for my share of food at Mom's."

"Nearly two years, right? That's too bad. Mom told me how much you loved the job; how Uncle Joe went to bat for you."

"Joe's a saint." That was how the conversation proceeded—curt and without much real meaning—until I blurted out "I'm thinking of coming to Ireland for a visit."

I discerned excitement—something that's highly unusual from my straight-forward, laid back, and open-as-a-book brother—in Augie's voice. "That would be lovely! We've got the extra bedroom. Aibreann and the wee one and I would love to have Uncle Neil come stay with us. The bed's yours for as long as you like."

I wiped a singular tear from my left eye and nodded, a gesture that my brother could not see. "How's little Caitlyn? I heard the delivery was rough and she was in the ICU for a couple of weeks."

There was a catch in Augie's reply, a sign that things had been precarious in the delivery room and thereafter. "She's perfect. Ten fingers and ten toes. Gaining weight. Smiling. Cooing like a pigeon in the park. Takes to the breast like one of those fat piglets you used to raise."

Augie's reference made me smile; again, not a gesture my brother, three thousand miles away in Ireland, could see. "I'd forgotten about those 4H pigs." I caught my breath, thought a bit, and blurted out an apology. "I should have called, about Caitlyn, I mean. Should have done what good brothers and uncles do. I'm sorry I didn't call before now."

"Not to worry. You had things to work out. Hell: I only called you the once to console you about your troubles. I've no standing to hold your silence against you." Augie paused again. "What say you, little brother? We've got the space and you've got the time. And there are openings at the factory where I work. I can put in a good word for you if you're intending to stay a bit." He took a breath, lowered his voice to a near whisper, as if Aibreann was in the room and he didn't want her to hear the rest. "If it's a matter of the airfare or the thousand pounds for the work permit ..."

"That's not it," I said, interrupting Augie before telling a lie.

I know Augie does well over there at his plastics company despite the recession, which ripped apart the Irish economy and put things in a tailspin for his firm; a company making plastic vents and baffles for British Minis. Car sales worldwide suffered. Remember what happened here? Obama stepped in and saved GM and Chrysler with bailouts. One of the best things he was allowed to do; but then, he had both the House and the Senate on his side. That was before Turtle Man took over. *Bah!* I think I despise that old coot more than I do the current guy in charge. *Whatever.* Augie's company came back strong once the economy picked up; after the EU propped up Greece and Spain and Iceland. Mom says my brother lost half his retirement in the downturn. Hope to hell he's getting some of it back. *Shit. He thinks I need a handout.* Nice of him to offer but Da didn't raise no fool. I have some savings. Living with Mom, taking odd jobs, I've been frugal, even in the throes of despondency. I can get my thin, boney ass over to Dublin, take the train to Athlone, and if I decide to stay, pay for my own damn work permit!

"Thanks, Augie but I'm good. I can swing the price of a two-way ticket to Dublin and train fare to Athlone."

"And then?"

"We'll see about the rest of it after I've been there a bit. It'll take me a week or so to get things set up. My passport's up to date. I'll fly Air Canada out of Winnipeg: It's cheaper than flying from the States. I think I can get Barbara to meet me at the airport, take the Dodge and store it. At least she's still talking to me."

The reality of the aftermath of the accident was that Barbara was the only member of the Prettyhorse/Comstock family who expressed empathy towards me when I sat in the last row at St. Peter's Episcopal in Warroad, an overflow crowd crammed into the pews, folks standing in the back of the church, fifty additional mourners seated in the adjacent social hall on folding chairs watching the funeral service on a flat screen. *What the hell did you expect? You killed three people and all three were eulogized during the service.* That's how I thought about what happened; the ugly reality of a two hundred ton locomotive smashing into a fragile pickup truck; no way to stop, no way to save the woman I loved or the children who were with her.

My mind eventually returned to the phone call. Augie was talking details, mentioning how Shannon Plastics had a dire need for workers, including mechanics, now that the recession had lifted, now that Cooper Minis were rolling off the floors of the Oxford manufacturing facility in England at the rate of a thousand cars a day.

"You're a decent mechanic, right?"

I worked the farm until Mom sold the place so I know my way around a wrench. There isn't much I can't fix. Though I'd never worked formally in a shop for pay, I can tear apart any motor or engine and rebuild it blindfolded. That's what Augie's leaving our farm really meant: It fell upon me to be Da's apprentice. "True, though I've never worked as such."

"Doesn't matter. I can sell it to the powers that be. Which means you can apply for a Skilled Worker's Employment Permit instead of a general. Much easier road to staying if that's what you decide."

"Okay," I said noncommittally.

Augie kept talking. "Every damn one of those cars needs what we make, Little Brother. There's a job here in Athlone for you if you want it. Wages aren't the best; twenty Euros an hour. But you can live rent free with us for the six month probationary period; longer if you need to. Aibreann's on board seeing as how I lied to her about how tidy and quiet you are!" He took a breath, or, given he's a chain smoker, more likely took a puff, probably having gone outside, away from his girlfriend and child to stand curbside to smoke. "Then there's the health care. At the wage I cited, you'll not be entitled to free care but it's relatively inexpensive to buy insurance and the company has a program of subsidizing those who need it. You'll find it easier and cheaper and, generally faster to get care here than in the States. Plus, there's profit sharing and a stock option program you can sign up for. You wouldn't get rich, Boyo, but you'd have a pretty damn good life."

The fact he used Da's label for me was endearing and, given the circumstances, made me break down and sob.

"There, there, Boyo. Mom shared the details of what happened. She also said there was nothing you could've done. Nothing. God doesn't provide all the answers and sometimes, He seems oblivious to our questions. No one will ever explain the 'why' behind what happened on that gravel road. But know this: You are loved—by your family and your friends—despite what occurred."

But not by Adeline's family—Barbara excepted. My big brother's voice, so calm, so restrained, so controlled was an echo of Da's. I wiped wetness from my cheeks with the cuff of my sleeve, the flannel quickly mopping up evidence of my upset. "Just a visit, Augie. I'm just coming for a visit. We'll see about the staying part after I've been there awhile"

"Okay."

Four months have transpired since that call. I came for a visit and stayed for the job Augustus offered. It's lovely living with my older brother and his family in their little townhouse just a stone's throw from the west bank of the Shannon. I'm starting to regain some of my confidence so that being alone, without others around, is less daunting, less taxing. I'll start looking for my own place next week. I've made the decision to seek permanent work status here. Maybe citizenship. Who knows? I mean, it's not like I give a good goddamn about what's going on back home. Things have gone to hell in a hand basket. I told you before; after the disappointment of the Obama years—not so much due to that part-Irish black man, who sought to bring hope to so many—but due to the failure of the American political system, I'm done voting. American politics is all about money and the big man. "Little fellas like us," as Da would say, "don't have a place at the table with the rich."

Spring has come. Flowers are blossoming and trees are leafing. Birds are in song, welcoming the warmth of the sun as it climbs higher into the bucolic Irish sky with each passing day. Augie has a boat—an ancient seventeen-foot, deep "v" wooden rower with an old Mercury thirty-horse outboard mounted on the stern—that he keeps on Lough Ree, the huge reservoir lake created by the impoundment of the Shannon, the longest river in Ireland. The lake's just north of town. Augie's taken me out on Lough Ree to chase brown trout and pike a couple of times and has promised to teach me how to fly fish. On our first outings, we were *technically* skunked; catching only rough fish—no keepers—and when we came back to

Aibreann and Caitlyn empty-handed after our day-long excursions, I heard Da's voice whispering in my head, lamenting he didn't do so well raising his boys given our failure at emulating James and John as fishermen.

Speaking of Saints, I've returned to the Catholicism of my youth, finding stability and solace in attending Saturday evening mass. We go to church as a family at the Cathedral of Sts. Peter and Paul. The church is but a stone's throw from my favorite watering hole—Sean's Bar—which, like most pubs in Ireland, claims to be the oldest place in the country to get a pint.

I sit in a pew with Augustus, Aibreann, and Caitlyn; Augie and Aibreann declining Eucharist due to their sins (cohabiting and procreating a child out of wedlock), circumstances—given the size of the congregation—the parish priests likely don't even appreciate. Still, Augie and Aibreann were raised Catholic. Testing the ire of the church by receiving the host in a state of sin (and possibly enduring eternal damnation) is not something Augustus Sean Donnelly or Aibreann Maria O'Connor are willing to risk. I take communion; they do not. That'll change once Augie proposes marriage (it's supposed to happen any day), Aibreann accepts (a certainty), and they tie the knot (guaranteed!).

The impending wedding of my older brother to his Irish lover evokes lamentation. The love unfolding between Augie and Aibreann, magnified and glorified by the affection they share for Caitlyn, reminds me of the path Adie and I had been walking. But then, as I reflect on the beauty that was once ours, I see reality as clear as my hands.

The horror usually haunts me at night, although I have no premonition as to when tribulation will strike. Yesterday I was underneath an extruding machine replacing a part on the pump that moves plastic through the mold when, without warning, nausea hit me. I wasn't physically ill. Only my spirit—my soul—was sickened. I have no earthly idea what triggered my malady. But there it was. I'll tell you what happened because it's only through telling I can lift the pall of that night and try to move ahead. My therapist has warned me not to verbalize my trauma. However, I've found that, in certain situations, recasting the nightmare in story makes it less ugly.

"Every time you recount what happened," Dr. Misty Nelson, the psychologist my medical doctor—Dr. Simonson, referred me to—warned, "you suffer additional harm."

I get what she's saying. I really do. The Easter following the accident, Mom and I were at St. Mary's Catholic Church in Warroad. We were sitting in the social hall after mass waiting for Easter brunch. Mom grew tired of well-meaning folks coming up to me, asking me how I was doing, obliquely prodding me for details of what happened. Mom got pissed (not a word she would use), stood up, clanged a spoon against her juice glass, and addressed her fellow parishioners.

"You keep asking Neil how he's doing, asking him for his version of what he went through that night. Well, you all know what happened. His train broadsided his fiancée's pickup truck. Three people died. It was a horrific, unavoidable tragedy. The police and the railroad investigated things and cleared Neil of any wrongdoing. But can you imagine how he feels? Killing the woman you love and two children? Watching it all happen and being absolutely unable to do one thing to stop it? Can you fathom how hard he hurts, how much this has cost him? You're all supposed to be Christians: For God's sake, show some Christian charity and leave my son alone!"

Emelia LaRoche Donnelly, whose voice had thundered upset, whose face had turned scarlet in anger, then sat down and calmly waited for her food. She'd come back from Hawaii, cutting her time in paradise short to be with me, to mother me despite the fact I was nearly thirty, after she heard the news. Given she's the largest tither to that little church, folks listened. The parishioners of St. Mary's left me alone.

I've gotta say: Misty's admonition still holds water. I suffer every time I retell the story. Still, I can't help myself. I feel driven to relate what took place. I don't understand why I must talk about something so horrific but I must.

I stared at the Mazda, the sky pouring golf balls of ice onto the tracks, the truck, and the land as a diminutive woman stood next to the rear door on the passenger's side, frantic and desperate to save the lives of those inside.

My God, I thought, *Chloe and Timmy are in the back seat!*

But, and this is likely the only positive thing that can be said about that night (if substituting one child's life for another's can ever be seen as positive) I was wrong about who was in the truck. Adie wasn't trying to free her own children: She was struggling to save her niece Abigail Anderson, who at two, was strapped in a car seat—making extraction all the more challenging—and her nephew Devon, age seven months, whose child carrier was also belted in. I didn't know this truth as my locomotive rounded the bend and approached the stricken truck at an angle—couldn't have, given the hail and the dark and the shock of the scene unfolding before my eyes. I learned it later, once I'd been given a preliminary breath test by a state trooper who was helping Lake of the Woods deputies with their investigation, once I'd been cleared of having *any* alcohol in my system. It was also after I'd given my statement in Baudette, pissed in a cup (the test showing I had no drugs in my system), and was being driven home by that same trooper when he filled me in. He was the one who told me who'd died. The deputies wouldn't let me near the crash site. I gave my first, informal statement at the scene before convulsing, retching, and tossing my cookies while standing next to the idling locomotive. Knowing that Adie's torn and battered body reposed in snow was bad enough. I didn't need to see her. I knew what had happened. The train came to a halt a quarter-mile past the accident scene; stopping far sooner than I expected but too late to save Adie and the kids. Tragedy tore my soul apart and shattered my resilience. *I killed a family,* I had thought. It was only in the state patrol cruiser heading home, three bodies left behind and covered by blankets, the investigation ongoing, when I learned I hadn't killed Adie's kids.

    You want to know what I see when the scene asserts itself? I see, of course, the night and the hail and the headlamp of the locomotive illuminating the stricken truck. I see Adie panicking, having trouble opening the truck's rear passenger door. I see the door opening and my fiancée leaning into the truck, her heroic efforts visible because the truck's dome light is on. I watch with unsupported hopefulness as Adeline lifts one child free of the truck. But then my optimism deflates, like a balloon pricked with a pin, when Adie runs behind the truck carrying that child in her arms—intent, I believe, on retrieving a second child. Then it happens: Adie slips and falls, clutching the child to her chest as she spills onto icy ground. Adie rises to her knees but the heaviness of the toddler in her arms and the slickness of the ground make it difficult for her to stand. By the time she's regained her footing, it's too late. The locomotive is upon her and Adie and the child are hit and tossed aside like rag dolls. *She could've saved herself,* I remember thinking as the unfathomable played out like a scene from a Stephen King novel. *She could've dropped the child and escaped!*

"Jesus!" Johnny exclaimed just before the locomotive tore into Adie, his face tortured in upset, "she's carrying a kid!"

I never replied. I never told Johnny Duggan about the other child I suspected was inside the Mazda. I thought the kids were Adie's. Despite the age disparities between Adie's children and Joan's children, the differences never registered. It was only on the ride home, when the trooper explained who was dead, that I came to know. I also never saw Joan and Doug Anderson pull up to the crossing in their Toyota after hearing the crash shortly after Adie left their place. They didn't know I was behind the controls of the locomotive when they arrived at the crossing. They learned that detail soon enough and immediately blamed me for what happened.

The truth is, when the trooper told me who'd died in the crash, I felt no relief. *Adeline and two children are gone,* I remember thinking, after he said what he said and the cruiser became silent save for the squawking of the shortwave. His revelation didn't ease my burden. Later on, as I reflected upon that night, the fact I did not kill Adie's children became a thin, fragile strand of something. Of what, to this day, I cannot say.

Chapter Thirteen

Ennistymon. I sit at the bar of The Falls Hotel, sipping my pint, the black stout and white froth expertly poured to separation by the comely lass tending bar, her eyes full of skepticism and scrutiny, the sort of nonchalant gaze bartenders must possess to retain sanctimony when regaled by drunkards. *Kate's eyes,* I think, pretending to study the cascading stout in my glass while casting sly glances at the pretty, amply chested, thickly-built barmaid close to my own age who seems bored with her lot in life as she works a crossword out of *The Irish Times* Saturday edition. My silent assessment is that the bartender looks a bit like Kate Winslet. Not the Kate of dyed red hair but the Kate of naturally blonde hair and blue eyes. Topaz blue—as I recall—alert, intelligent, and clairvoyant just like this Irish girl's eyes. Both the bartender and Kate are fair skinned and their lovely faces are free of blemish. The bartender leans over the bar. The sleeves of her blouse rest on the varnished oak surface. She remains oblivious to me and hard at work on her puzzle. Her eyes avoid mine. The eraser of a yellow pencil is clamped between ample, though not too large, teeth in concentration. Augie is off elsewhere looking for a fishing guide, someone who knows the ins and outs of the fall migration of salmon from the Atlantic up the Inagh.

    Augie's bound and determined to teach me how to catch Atlantic salmon with wet flies. "That's the only way to river fish," he's said more than once during my year in Ireland. "A long pole, a crank reel, flies, a creel, waders, and the grip of an Irish river, Boyo," he's fond of saying, working me, trying to convert me.

    After we were routinely skunked fishing Lough Ree, we hired a guide. Then we caught fish. After a few guided trips—having found the best places to troll and cast—now it's just Augie and me, and, on occasion, Aibreann and the little one; all of us wearing life jackets to set a good example for the child as we fish out of the wooden boat, the Mercury outboard coughing oily smoke, my brother, despite his income, too damn cheap to ditch a perfectly good two-stroke for a cleaner, quieter four-stroke.

    The fish dinners my sister-in-law fries up (you caught that, eh? ... the fact that Augie and Aibreann are now good-to-go in terms of receiving the Eucharist!) are beyond splendid. She's a phenomenal cook and, once she and Augie have decided how big their family should be (she says two, he says three kiddos) she'll likely go back to being a chef at some eatery in Athlone. That's how she and Augie met: She was the cook at his favorite breakfast place, a dive where her excellence in the kitchen was underutilized. During fishing trips to Lough Ree without Aibreann, Augie muses he might spring free some cash from his tight fists to buy one of the posher establishments in town and install his beloved as head chef. "Fantastic idea," has been my constant refrain when the idea is posited. "She's got a gift, she does," I always add.

As the bartender works her crossword, I reach into a pocket of my fishing jacket, pull out an envelope, open it, and remove a wrinkled letter. It's not like I don't know what it says. I've read the letter a half-dozen times since Barbara Comstock wrote me.

Winnipeg, Manitoba
September 11, 2018

Dear Neil:

I'm hopeful that some of your despair and sadness and yes, guilt, over the accident has abated. It's been three years since Adeline and the children passed and I know, at least for me, it isn't all that much easier. But there is hope, right? I mean, all we can do is get along, moving one foot ahead of the other, trying to live out our lives as Adie would want us to. I pray that's what you are trying to do over there in Ireland.

Your mother shared with me the photos from Augustus's and Aibreann's wedding. What a lovely couple! The face of their dear one brought tears to my eyes: She looks so much like Joanie's little boy; it's a shock to see such a resemblance since there is no familial relationship between the two children; one here, one gone to the Father. Have you noticed this coincidence? I bet you have. Enjoy Caitlyn, Neil, despite whatever bad memories her face may trigger. She is surely a gift from God.

Sadly, I must bring you additional bad news: Dave will not let it go. It's not Joanie who's behind what's happening but that damned, good-for-nothing son-in-law of mine. Nearly three years after the tragedy, he's still blaming you for what happened. I've tried talking to him but he's an idiot and a vengeful idiot at that. He's hired a lawyer from Duluth to bring a wrongful death suit against the CN.

That's fine if he wants to do that and claim the railroad was negligent in its maintenance of that godawful crossing. But, and here's the part that irks me, he's also insisting on naming you as a defendant. Suing you, and the CN as your employer, for negligence. Claims you could have avoided the accident. Claims you were asleep at the controls. Your conductor that night, Johnny Duggan, is supporting Dave's case. Says he saw you dozing off right before the accident. That's not what he told the deputies: His statement at the time, that you were alert and tried to do everything in your power to stop the train, is in writing. So you might ask, "Why the change in story?" Well, I can only speculate, but it's come to light that Duggan's wife is cousins with the Anderson clan. Blood being thicker than water, Johnny has decided to lie. That's the long and short of it. I'm told by your mother that the suit papers will be served on you within the month. I've run this whole sorry mess by my personal attorney in Warroad, Elmer Pratt. You and Adie were in school with his son, Jamie, remember? That really fat kid with acne? I think he was in Adie's class. Anyway, Elmer says the suit, which is venued in Roseau County, won't survive the railroad's motion to dismiss. Elmer also says, "Tell Neil not to worry. The CN will pay for his defense. Protocol, you know." But I thought you should be aware that your label for my son-in-law, "Dipshit Dave," is something I have adopted given his stupidity. Joanie is not on board with this but, as she is still torn apart by grief, has neither the gumption to stop the suit nor leave the asshole. Sorry about the language. A writer should be able to use more refined words. But he is most completely and decidedly an asshole.

  There is one small positive that has come out of all this. Adie's passing, as tragic as it is, knocked the snot out of Amos. It's no secret that Adeline is his favorite. Oh, he loves all four, don't worry about that. But Adie? She has a special place in Amos's heart. I figured that her death would send him over the edge, into the abyss. But instead, he looked around, saw the beauty of his remaining family, and pulled his head out of his ass. The long and short of it is that he hasn't had a drink in nine months. He's been battling; it took three stints at rehab to get this far. But I think that old Ojibwe will make it! We've stayed together, me living my life in Winnipeg, him running the resort with Eleanor's help. But things are better. I'm considering selling my condo and moving back to the Angle. Time will tell if that reunion comes to fruition or not.

I want to close as I opened by telling you: I've never blamed you for what happened. I know how much you loved—no, that's not right—love Adeline. I've spoken with Chloe's and Timmy's fathers and very soon, the kids will write to you. I've also got Amos turned around: He's no longer asking for your head on a spike. I've made him, and our other kids (Joanie, despite her loss, <u>never</u> really blamed you!) see the light. There's more healing to be done; more work ahead. But I'll do it, Neil. Why? Because Adie and her kids adore you, that's why. And I do too!

I hope to be able to visit Athlone with Chloe and Timmy next summer. Their fathers are in agreement and have applied for passports for the kids. It's time everyone leave things that are in the past alone. It's a tall order, I know. Adie's kids have been poisoned by family rumors and untoward remarks about you. But I'm doing what I can to fix that.

Until then ...
Lovingly,
Barbara
PS ... Your mom left Leala with Amos while she's travelling. My unsentimental, sparse-with-his-words husband has fallen in love with your Brittany. In fact, he's trained her to point and just yesterday, she retrieved her first ruffed grouse! I'm hoping you'll let her stay at the resort instead of being cooped up at your mom's house in Warroad. Let me know if that's OK with you. She's an amazingly kind animal and is already head and shoulders above any other dog Amos has ever owned or hunted over.

"What's wrong?"

The bartender puts down her pencil and watches my tears drip onto the letter. Unintended moisture causes the ink of Barbara's sentiments to bleed black. I grab a linen napkin from the bar and wipe my cheeks before placing the letter back in its envelope and tucking it into a pocket of my fishing vest. A not-so-subtle change comes over the bartender. The skepticism and defensiveness that had been present when she slid the first pint of Beamish towards me—her façade a measure of security and protection against untoward male patrons—is gone. I shake my head, take a sip of stout, and pull together enough wherewithal to force a weak smile. That line from *Revolutionary Road*, a line Adie had objected to—April's statement to Frank that, "We were never destined to be great or special,"—plays in my head as I try to hide my grief from a stranger. "It's nothing."

The lass, her crystal blue eyes locked on my *faux* smile, shakes her head. "A bartender always knows when a patron is fibbing." That makes me laugh. "You're like a therapist. You know when someone's holding back."

Her wide face breaks into a radiant smile, exposing a silver filling covering one of her incisors. The metal glints as it catches light. "Right. Just like a shrink, you can tell me anything! What's your name, anyway?"

"Neil. Neil Donnelly."

"American?"

"Not for long. I work in Athlone. As a mechanic. I'm applying for naturalization."

"No shit?" Genuine interest overcomes the woman's native defensiveness. Her sincerity and effervescence obviate my guilt, my shame, my sorrow.

"No shit."

She nods at my empty glass. "Another?"

"Sure."

She pours a second Beamish. "There's a story behind that, I'll wager. Both how you came to be in Athlone and what's in that letter." She lets the stout settle before finishing the pour. "Care to tell it to me?" she asks, sliding the glass to me, her topaz eyes earnest in their appreciation for my plight, a situation she seems to perceive but cannot begin to know. "I'm a very good listener."

I slurp foam from the top of the pint. "Can't do that until I know your name and we've been properly introduced," I say, extending my right hand.

"Fallon. Fallon Saoirse O'Reardon," she says, shaking my hand. Her fingers are long, thin, soft, and dry. Mine are nearly identical in length but wider, calloused, and sweaty from nerves.

"Interesting middle name. Irish?"

"T'is. Was my maternal grandmother's name. It means 'freedom'."

I relax. "Da was a Michael Collins fan. Seems freedom, at least the dream of it, is a very Irish notion. His parents came to the States from Athlone. He was born in the States but he never lost the lilt."

"The movie sucked."

"Oh?" I sense something is amiss. It's like the small perch of rapport we've built is slipping underfoot. But like Adie and Barbara—maybe it's not magic, maybe it's because I'm an open book—Fallon's able to read me and correct my misconception.

"You've not upset me. I'm a Collins fan like your Da. Irish freedom means everything. It's God and Country. Right? It's just the movie didn't get all of it right, is all. The Troubles, I mean."

I nod again, though I have no earthly idea what the hell she's talking about. "And Fallon? What's it mean?"

She winks. "The one in charge!"

I laugh. "I should've guessed."

No one else enters the pub on this rainy, dreary September afternoon. The hotel's guests are holed up in their rooms or braving bus excursions to the Cliffs of Mohr or shopping in Limerick. As I struggle to keep our connection alive, really the first intelligent, thoughtful, kind conversation I've had with a woman my own age since the accident, I peek at Fallon's left hand.

She notes my surreptitious glance and shakes her head. "I'm not spoken for. Was, up until a month ago. Wedding date was set and all that. But," she pauses and pats the back of my hand, "before I tell you *my* story, you need to tell me yours."

Augie couldn't find a guide. When he finally shows and I say a respectful goodbye to Fallon, my brother and I leave The Falls Hotel, drive west to where we think the salmon *might* be, park the decrepit forty-year-old Morris Minor Augie insists on driving despite having a shitload in the bank, slip on waders, attach flies to our lines, and clamber down the banks of the Inagh in a light drizzle to try our luck.

As I stand in slippery water attempting to replicate the arc of the fly fisherman's cast Augie has drilled into my head after forcing me to watch *A River Runs Through It* four times, Adie demands my attention. Her insistence on being with me, given I have a slip of paper with Fallon O'Reardon's telephone number and email tucked inside my wallet, is unnerving. But for the first time since the accident I discern Adie isn't asking me to relive those final, panicked moments leading up to her death. Instead, she looks at me from The Beyond with kindness. Then she whispers: Her voice—raspy, clear, and full of caring—haunts me as I attempt to replicate the casts Augie is making upstream. Try as I might, I can't capture the to and fro, the angle of rod and the rhythm of line cutting the wet Irish air my older brother has perfected.

The Inagh swirls around my thighs. Icy, clairvoyant water roils to the sea. I fish in a mist-filled valley beneath a gently weeping sky and Adie releases me from stricture born of tragedy.

"We *were* special and we *were* great," Adie laments, "and it's not your fault we are no longer so."

The End

More Short Stories

Threshold

I'll be honest. The last place I expected to end up this afternoon was the Anchor Bar. It's not wise. No, that's too tentative a word. It's not prudent for me to be standing at the threshold of one of the places that laid me low. Still, here I am. Go figure. Late autumn sun backlights me in silhouette as I ponder the situation. *You go in,* I say to myself, *you walk over and talk to Connie and the whole damn business will start all over again.*

Connie is my wife. I'd like to say, my ex. But there's no truth behind that, no legality to the statement though we've gone our separate ways. My stuff is my stuff and hers is hers. We haven't made love in over eight years, after one last drunken pratfall into bed together. Satisfying? Hardly. Quick. Painless. Without consequences. Hell, after all, we're married so there was no sin to the thing. And certainly no harm to anyone outside of our weird little dance. She lives in Superior. I live, or should say lived, at the Kozy—across the bay in Duluth. Until the damn place went up in flames after some bastard fell asleep with a cigarette in bed. Some say it's not much of a loss, having the Kozy burn down. Those folks didn't live there, didn't need the cheap rent like me and the others who called the run down, vermin-infested old building home. For a while, when I was getting my bearings after the fire, I caught a night here and there with friends, sleeping on couches. Then I found another place to live. I use my VA and Social Security money to buy groceries and take care of a few bills. Since drying out three years back, I haven't had to worry about wasting what little I've got on booze. But now, standing in the autumn breeze, looking into the dimness of the Anchor, an old fear, the fear of failure, wafts over me like smoke drifting over a camper at a campfire.

Connie tilts her head at me in that critical way she has about her. I can see her drink—a rum and Coke—in the dim light of the dark bar. The amber of the booze and the dark syrup of the soft drink aren't mixed very well: The booze is floating near the brim of the glass. *If she doesn't stir that,* I think, *her first sip will be a doozy.*

I know this about my wife: She doesn't drink cheap. There's no bar booze in that glass. It's top shelf Jamaican sitting in front of her. That's a certainty; a truth you can take to the bank.

I'm nervous as I stand in the open doorway, cool air migrating into the warmth of the room. My hand is poised at the right pocket of my blue jeans where I keep my wallet. The back fusion, the result of my helicopter gunship being shot down by a Viet Cong RPG (in my very first battle as a machine gunner on a Huey) and the resultant crushing of nearly every vertebra in my spine when the chopper crashed, prevents me from keeping a wallet in my back pocket.

Pain. There's always pain.

"Hello, Max," Connie says, her words clear, alcohol not yet coloring her enunciation. "It's been a long time."

I'm a little surprised. Normally, by this time of day, Connie is slurring her words, spilling drinks, and making goo-goo eyes at any guy within ten feet of her. It's a good sign that she's still standing at the bar rail and not sitting on a stool. She *seems* sober, capable of understanding what it is I have to tell her.

I remain at the threshold. Part of me wants to go back to who I was, what we had: that soft, velvety high of near constant inebriation we shared for the twenty-seven years we were together.

Twenty-seven years. Three kids. A son and two daughters. Kyle, Lila, and Jennifer. Despite our failings, despite foreclosure, bankruptcy, my two DUI's, and Connie's felony conviction for stealing from the Red Cross (she managed the charity's pull-tab operations in three bars including the Anchor) our kids have stayed out of trouble. It helps that not a one of them is a drunk. Or an addict. Or a thief.

"We need to talk," I say in as deferential a voice as I can muster.

"Come on over and have a bump with me," my wife says invitingly, pointing to an empty stool.

Connie knows me. Knows my whole unattractive history. The rages. The fists through television screens and windows. My attempts to medicate the constant aching of my spine—a mess of rods and screws and wires that some Army surgeon in Saigon cobbled together like a Rube Goldberg device to keep me upright—with prescription pain killers chased by straight bourbon. The raised voice. The stormy temper. Oh, Connie knows me all right, and despite it all, despite the distance we've forced upon ourselves, still loves me.

But Connie also knows that I've been sober for three solid years. Three years of daily struggle, living in an apartment above a bar, resisting the warm glow of whiskey that, on a nightly basis, called to me from beneath the moldy floorboards of the Kozy like some Siren beckoning a lovesick sailor.

Damn you, Connie Sturgis. Damn you to hell.
My right hand twitches. Fingers strain against denim. I ball my left hand into a fist. Not as a threat but in an attempt to control my anxiety.

I look around. The other patrons, two men I don't know and who are too young and far too good looking to be interested in my wife, sit at the bar and sip flat tap beer from murky glasses, their conversation muted and unintelligible as I consider my next move.

"What's wrong, Max? You turning all shy and thoughtful on me in your old age?" Connie says coyly before taking a hefty slurp from her drink.

My right hand leaves the safety of my jean pocket and adjusts the Stetson on my head so I can look at my wife without obstruction.

"Nice to see you too," I say quietly, walking into the bar.

I find space to the right of Connie and stand next to her. *She's gained weight,* I think, studying her as her pale gray eyes study me.

She raises her drink to her lips, lips that, when we were young lovers, did things with me and to me that no other woman has ever done. Uncharacteristically, she's not wearing lipstick. There's a hint of rouge on her cheeks and the standard bright blue eyeliner she always wears below her eyebrows. But there's no lipstick.

"You don't like me much, do you?" she asks, returning to the familiar, exhausting dialogue that eventually wore me out and caused me to leave.

I look away, feigning interest in a college football game, the Gophers and the Badgers, on the flat screen behind the bar.

Angela, the bartender, a woman a few years younger than me and a high school classmate of Connie's from Superior High School, slides over and gives me a nod.

"Haven't seen you in here in a long while," Angie says, the wear of years of bartending in a rough neighborhood of a rough town etched on her face. "What'llyahave?"

The question comes out as a single word. I bite my lip. Connie is waiting for an answer to her question but, with Angie standing across from us, it's not the time to engage my wife.

"Sprite, if you got it."

"7 Up OK?"

I glance at Angie. There are age lines around her eyes; small, slight, almost Asian slits of blue; and around the corners of her mouth. But beyond that, in comparison to Connie, who has ballooned to a weight she never saw during her pregnancies, Angie Marquart is in great shape. Her breasts sit, not like Connie's, poised for collapse to the floor, but high and perky. I discern nipples through her blouse and bra and her cleavage strikes me as inviting. I know, from a romp or two with Angie years back, that she's a distance runner; that she stays in great shape. She's also sober, ten years or better. And single; a facet of her situation I never acted upon.

Maybe it could have worked.

"That'll do," I finally answer.

She pats the back of my hand like a parent approving a child and moves deftly towards the soda guns at the end of the bar.

Probably for the best I never made a serious move. She's got her shit together, that girl. Why draw her into my hell?

"You are *so* obvious," Connie mumbles.

I sense my wife's mood shift. There's more than mere observation in my wife's words. I know her too well. I can hear the needle of criticism, the adjective "fuckin'" unspoken but lingering before "obvious" in the sentence, as she slams the base of her empty glass against varnished pine.

"Calm down," I say quietly.

Connie's eyes, the same eyes that once looked up at me in ecstasy from our marital bed, lock on mine. There is no love in those eyes now as she considers my appreciation of Angie at her expense.

"Fuck you."

There it is. The alcohol has freed Connie to be who she really is—a mean-spirited drunk who has lost it all. But then, isn't that who I was? At least, before my last month-long stay in the local spin-dry, my fourth trip to treatment, the visit that finally brought me freedom. I study the woman who gave me three beautiful children, kids who, as I've said, have done all right for themselves despite Connie and me. It's tough, thinking about them at a time like this, with what I have to tell my wife. But there's pride in the knowing, in the appreciation of them. Not even Connie's foul mouth can diminish my fondness for our kids.

After my last CD treatment, I was able to find a part-time job at the Duluth YMCA working with children of color in the Central Hillside as a mentor in math and English. It's ten bucks an hour, twenty hours a week. The gig's enough for me to reclaim some sense of self-worth; something I hadn't possessed since 'Nam. The pay is small enough it doesn't impact my VA benefits or my Social Security Disability. Plus, with my three kids grown and gone from the Twin Ports (wisely leaving behind their wreck of a family to make their own ways) I kind of like being around children. Keeps me optimistic, if you know what I mean.

"There's no need to swear," I say to Connie.

Angie brings me the Sprite and slides another drink in front of Connie.

I was wrong, I think, studying the bloated, blotchy face of my wife. *She's already toasted. I guess she's getting better at holding her booze.*

Connie swigs from her glass and stares at me. "Why the fuck are you here? I don't need a fuckin' sermon, if that's what this is about. I don't need you all sober and righteous telling me how to live my life. Is that why you're here, Max? To preach to me?"

The weight of knowing what I know presses down on me. I've been dreading this moment since yesterday, when I answered the door of the little efficiency I'm living in at the Seaway Hotel in Duluth's seedy West End. It's all I can do to look at the woman I once loved, who, in some ways, will always be part of who I was, who I am. I gulp air. The room spins.

Kyle didn't ask. He is, after all, twenty-three years old, old enough to make his own decisions, old enough to choose his own path. Laid off from his job at the foundry he worked at in St. Paul (he was one hell of a welder, I'm told), with one kid at home, a pretty Hispanic wife (Rita, a girl I met only once, at their wedding) carrying their second, Kyle felt he'd run out of options. Growing up in our home Kyle learned early on what kind of hell breaks loose when a repo man shows up with a tow truck for the family van; when bills sit on the kitchen counter because there's no money to pay for bad habits. He didn't want that for his wife, a girl he cherished so much you could see love cascading off Kyle's face like glory light in a religious icon whenever Rita is present. He didn't want that for his daughter, Hester, or the second child about to be. We didn't talk about these things; not at all, not since the wedding. But I know Kyle: I know how his mind works.

Worked. Past tense.

Had he asked, I would have told him there are other options, other ways to make a go of it. But he is, was, a stubborn kid. A good kid, though pigheaded like his mom. He wouldn't have listened; not to me, his often-drunk daddy who once hit Kyle so hard in a fit of stupid, alcohol-induced rage I put him through a screen door. Sobriety didn't heal that wound or the many others incurred by Kyle and his older sisters. Still, I wish he had asked.

"Something's happened," I say, my eyes focused on the game on the bar television, cowardice preventing me from delivering the news candidly, like a man should.

I remember Connie at Kyle's wedding. A joyous affair in St. Paul. Rita's family didn't have much, being they were recent immigrants to the States from Mexico and all. But the church wedding was beautiful. The bride was a quintessential study in Latin grace and elegance. Her dark skin was set off by the pristine white of her wedding gown; her raven hair tied up; not even a hint of her pregnancy with Hester to be detected in her slender waist. The reception at the local Knights of Columbus overlooking the Mississippi went without a hitch mainly because Connie, my once-beautiful wife, had pulled herself together and remained sober for probably the first time since puberty. She drank straight Coke all night long and acted the part of the groom's dutiful mother. I was so damned proud of her. That night, the thought occurred to me as I drove Connie to the Super 8 we both were staying at (in separate rooms), that maybe, just maybe she too could kick the booze. But as soon as Connie was back in her room with the door still ajar and me standing expectantly at the threshold, she was into the mini-fridge, mixing herself a rum and Coke, and offering me the chance to undo my recently-achieved sobriety. Didn't happen. I kissed her cheek, said goodnight, and left. I won't say it was easy. She looked splendid that night in her expensive, low-cut gown, her mature breasts hoisted into place and forming a welcoming "v" of flesh that, since I hadn't been with a woman in months, got my undivided attention despite our history. But I resisted Connie and the promise of steady nerves that a first drink would have provided. Until today, until I walked into the Anchor, Kyle's wedding night was the last time I'd seen her. The contrast between the woman I left in that motel room and the woman standing next to me today, well, it's remarkably sad.

"What are you babbling about? What's happened?" she asks. Connie's attitude has become *an* attitude.

I drain my soda, take a deep breath, and begin to tell.

"A captain and a master sergeant from the Marine Corps Recruiting Office came to my apartment yesterday ..."

Isle Royale

The twenty-two footer—an ancient Johnson outboard wheezing on idle, the impeller pushing thirty-five degree water—rolled in swells. A cloud of herring gulls settled next to the boat, their excited calls drawing more and more of their kind to the expected feast. The boat was anchored. Over a hundred feet of hemp rope, weathered by use, secured to a brass fitting bolted to the bow of the wooden boat by a double half-hitch, ran taut between the skiff and a seventy pound stainless steel Danforth. The anchor secured the *Miss Sky* in place against a nor'easter. Another two hundred feet of rope lay coiled in the bottom of the boat. The fisherman leaned into the starboard gunwale, his yellow rain gear glistening from spray, cold water dripping from his Twins ball cap as he pulled in the gill net, three hundred feet of synthetic rope, clear monofilament mesh, plastic floats, and lead weights stretched out across the reef north of Fisherman's Home along the eastern shore of the big island. He was after cisco, wistfully named "lake herring" by his Norwegian forefathers, men of unfailing courage who'd worked the waters of Isle Royale for generations before him. As the fisherman hauled in the net he felt the telltale weight of fish. It would be a good day. A very good day.

Everlasting Sky Oulette Thompson moved deliberately around a two-room cottage on Wright Island. Her husband, Kjell—three years her junior—had taken a semester off from his pre-med studies at Lakehead in Thunder Bay and was out on the water pulling nets; a trade he'd learned as a kid working alongside his cousins—the Rude boys—whose family held the lease at Fisherman's Home seven miles south of the Thompson camp. Sky—who never went by her first name—knew her determined Norwegian Irish husband—Kjell's maternal side plain in his flaming red hair, blue eyes, and freckled face—would be in the skiff he'd named for his wife fishing shoals off Long Island. If he was lucky, if the winds and the currents and Superior's zooplankton cooperated, fish would amass along the submerged reef running from Fisherman's Home to Menagerie Island and Kjell would fill his boat with herring.

Sky had been fishing with her husband and had, as a young girl, fished with her Ojibwe father, He-Who-Shouts-at-Rain Oulette, called "Herman" by the *gichi-mookomaan* (white men) he worked with in Grand Marais, Minnesota. Herman had recently been hired as a manager by Kwik Trip to run a new store being built in the Norwegian fishing village-turned-tourist trap. Herman still fished the big lake but favored a tug: an enclosed vessel powered by twin screws and matching 300 hp Cummins diesels, a boat considerably larger than *Miss Sky*.

The option to process herring from the stable, thirty-five-foot length of a fishing tug wasn't available to Kjell. The *Miss Sky*, formerly known as the *Island Belle*, a name Oscar Thompson (Kjell's paternal grandfather) had chosen when he built the boat from North Shore white pine back in the '40s, was handed down from Oscar to Dalmar—Kjell's father. The boat and the lease rights to Wright Island were Dalmar's inheritance from Grandpa Oscar, a man who spent more time *thinking* about looking for work and *thinking* about fishing than *doing* either. Though seemingly timeless, the Thompson camp exists on borrowed time: The buildings will be demolished and the island returned to wilderness when Dalmar, the last of the Thompsons alive the year Isle Royale became a National Park, passes away.

Sky stepped lightly despite pregnancy. The woman moved about the main room of the Thompson cottage, a ten by sixteen foot space including a sink, a white porcelain countertop, shelves holding staples, dishes, pots, pans and bins of utensils, a Torrid Windsor wood cook stove, a hide-a-bed couch, two overstuffed chairs, and a white and red stainless steel and porcelain topped table with matching chairs, without distress. The board and batten walls—built with lumber hauled from the mainland—lacked insulation. Sky stood in the doorway leading to the cabin's tiny bedroom. A bed and dresser were crammed into the space. She walked to a window and pushed aside a curtain. Sunlight played across a shabby quilt covering the bed. It was late September. Despite morning frost painting the ground, biting flies and mosquitoes would stir when the day warmed.

Sky left the bedroom to stand in front of a bank of windows overlooking the front lawn. She studied the dock, the fish house, and the sauna at the end of the dock. Sky's tawny face erupted in a smile as she watched a red squirrel, a constant companion she'd named *maji-manidoo* (devil), scamper over the camp's picnic table. The grass remained green despite the onset of fall. The bay rippled and lapped against stones three generations of Thompsons had placed along the shoreline. *Maji-manidoo* skittered across the table, stood on its hind legs, and scolded the pregnant woman.

"Ha," Sky said, small, coffee-stained teeth clicking as she spoke, "so you're hungry, eh?" The woman moved towards a sack of sunflower seeds sitting on the floor, opened the sack, and scooped seeds with a cup. Carrying the cup brimming with seeds in her right hand, Sky snatched a coffee mug—steam rising against morning—with her left and moved towards the front door.

Bang.

The screen door slammed behind Sky. She set the coffee mug on the picnic table and dumped the sunflower seeds into a bird feeder. The squirrel's expectant eyes glistened. "OK, little one, eat," Sky whispered. The squirrel ran across the table and climbed a steel pole to reach the feeder. Sunflower seeds scattered as the rodent shoved food into its mouth. "Hey! Leave some for the chickadees!"

Honor, the name they'd picked for the baby, kicked. "Ouch!" Sky cried, rubbing her rounded belly. "Damn it, Honor, that hurt." The woman claimed a bench. The baby quieted. Sky Thompson sipped warm coffee and noted heavy weather closing from the east.

The second lift brought in seventy-five pounds of herring; silvery fish caught by their gills in the netting. Kjell pulled herring free of monofilament, poked holes in their bellies with a fillet knife to release air, and tossed the fish into plastic bins. Back on Wright Island, Kjell would gut the herring and the occasional lake trout, wash the fish, and repack the bins with ice for the trip to the mainland.

When Kjell was not in school, he and Sky shared the Thompson family home on Devils Track Lake with Kjell's parents, Dalmar and Celine. In Thunder Bay, Kjell and Sky rented an apartment near the Lakehead campus. During winter break Kjell would gather his buddies to cut ice on Devils Track Lake. Though Dalmar had taught Kjell how to harvest ice, Dalmar no longer assisted his son in cutting or transporting the ice from the mainland to Wright Island on Dalmar's thirty-foot Bertram.

Dalmar bought the Bertram years ago and operated it sparingly, having spent—in his estimation—too much time on the cold waters of Superior witnessing his father drink cheap beer and curse bad luck. Though Dalmar was outwardly unaffectionate, he was generous with his possessions. As a kid, Kjell ran the Bertram—a twin-engined deep water boat—up and down the North Shore before he was old enough to drive a car. Because Dalmar had little interest in the

Bertram, it bore the name it came with, a name of no significance to the Thompson family—*The Burbot.*

Kjell knew that this would be his last season pulling nets. *There's the baby,* Kjell thought, tossing herring into one bin, lake trout in another. *And Sky's career. She was picked to be the Park's artist in residence. Her watercolors are fantastic: She captures the essence of this place.* Kjell glanced up, his rubber gloves covered in blood, and noted a change in the weather. The idling outboard coughed. Then died. "That doesn't look good," the fisherman said, watching a black sky manifest. Gauging the distance to the incoming squall, Kjell calculated he had ten minutes to finish his work. *Anyway: This is it. I'll put up the skiff, close up camp and, if and when we get back here, I'll toss a hook and a smelt out into Siskiwit for lakers, watch Honor grow, and make love to Sky. Maybe make Honor a brother or a sister. Being the only one sucks. Honor will need a sibling and Sky and I need to slow things down. Medical school's taking too much out of me. It's time to admit I can't make amends for Grandpa's poor reputation as a fisherman. The Angry Trout and the Vanilla Bean and the Lemon Wolf can find herring elsewhere: There are plenty of fishermen who can supply fish. This is it,* Kjell Thompson thought as he drew the last of the netting into the skiff, *the last season.*

The wind ramped up as Sky removed laundry from a clothesline. Cumulus clouds stacked from water to sky and obliterated the blue that once stood above the Menagerie Island lighthouse three miles to the east. The gale bent hundred-year-old spruce. Lightning flashed. Thunder rolled. Sky tossed laundry into a wicker basket and scrambled into the cabin just as the storm let loose.

"Goddamnit," she cried, "where the hell is Kjell?" Sky stared out a rain-streaked window and witnessed weather lift her painter's easel and a watercolor-in-progress from the front lawn and smash it against the trunk of a white cedar. The painting destroyed, her attention reverted to consideration of her husband. "I hope to God he's not out in this shit."

Kjell pushed the "start" button on the Johnson and heard a faint "click". The battery was dead. Rain dripped from the brim of his cap as Kjell considered his next move. Warm water washed Kjell's face as he stood up in the skiff, opened a toolbox, removed a length of rope, unlatched the outboard's cowling, set the fiberglass cowling in the bottom of the boat, wound the rope around the flywheel, and yanked. The combination of Kjell pulling on the rope and a rogue wave tossed him overboard. Kjell immediately knew he was in trouble. He wasn't wearing a life jacket. His rubber boots and raingear weighed him down. The lake was near freezing. The waves were six feet high. And then, the boat's anchor broke free of its mooring.

Damn that was stupid, Kjell thought, removing his left boot as he tread water. *Good thing I wore wool longies,* he continued, prying off his right boot. *Wool has insulation value even when wet, though,* he admitted, drawing upon knowledge gained by a lifetime spent on the Big Lake, *hypothermia comes on fast. Damn it to hell,* the cuss rolled through Kjell's mind, *the boat is drifting away. No chance to swim for it. It won't be long before I shut down.* Kjell's raingear—filled with air and acting as a life preserver—kept his head above water. And then, as an enormous whitecap lifted Kjell high into the air, the fisherman perceived salvation.

When her husband didn't return, Sky Thompson keyed up the camp's satellite phone. Because it was autumn, the park rangers had shuttered the Malone Bay station and moved to Rock Harbor at the far north end of the big island.

"He's never been caught out in something like this," Sky said in as even a voice as she could muster.

"Where was he fishing?" Ranger Beth Evans asked.

The women had met once when Sky was running an art program for tourists at Rock Harbor Lodge. From that singular encounter, Sky knew Beth Evans was a no-nonsense woman. "Off Long Island. His nets run from Fisherman's Home to Menagerie."

"The *Voyageur II* is ready to return to Grand Portage. Hjalmar Johnson's skippering today. Good guy. I can get him to take a look. I'll notify the Coast Guard but in this shit, it'll take 'em a long time to get out here from the mainland." The ranger stopped and thought further. "I'll catch a ride with Hjalmar and bring some folks with. The more eyes the better."

"How soon can you leave? It's getting nastier by the minute!" Sky shouted, anxiety breaking through.

"Ten minutes tops. The boat's fueled and ready to go. With the wind at our back, we can be at Menagerie Island inside the hour."

An hour? God, he won't last ten minutes! Wait. I don't know he's in the water. He grew up on the island. Being out in rough weather is nothing new to Kjell. Sky sat at the kitchen table, rain pounding the metal roof of the cabin, and reached for a tissue. She dabbed her eyes and considered the solid, unrelenting persistence defining her husband. *When we're having a disagreement, those traits can be so aggravating. But in this case, stubborn resolve may save his life.* "Thank you, Beth. Hurry, will ya?"

"I'm out the door."

There was danger lurking around the rocky reefs stretching from Glenlyon Shoal to Fisherman's Home. Though only a few acres of Menagerie Island rise above Lake Superior's surface, a hull-cracking shelf surrounding the island extends in all directions. The lighthouse, standing sixty feet above the barren islet, is painted white while the keeper's house retains the raw red of its sandstone brick construction. The light was automated in 1913. As a consequence, no keeper occupies the residence. Access to the island is difficult: The rock shelf sloping from the lighthouse to the lake ends in a stone outcropping that—when the lake is angry—is as slippery as an eel.

"We should be coming up on it!" Beth Evans shouted. Beth and two other rangers stood at the stainless steel railing of the *Voyageur II* scanning the lake. "The light should be on but I can't make it out. Can either of you see anything through this soup?"

A tall, thin ranger—his body covered in bright yellow raingear—shook his head. His partner, a short, squat ranger covered in identical foul weather gear, scanned tempestuous water with binoculars. "There it is! Starboard, a hundred yards out."

"Captain," Evans yelled over the wind. "Slow 'er down. We're closing on the island."

Hjalmar Johnson heard Evans through an open window of the boat's cockpit. "I see Thompson's skiff," Johnson yelled back. "Looks to be taking on water." Fifty yards ahead of the trawler, the *Miss Sky*, its gunwales nearly submerged, waves pounding the water-laden craft against rocks, floated marginally in the storm. "Don't see anyone in 'er, though."

"How close can you get?"

"This is about it," Johnson shouted, struggling to maintain the position of the boat by adjusting power to the screws. "You'll need to use the Zodiac to get closer."

"Casperson, come with me. Life jacket on. Nelson, you stay put."

Casperson—the shorter of the other two rangers—and Evans donned life jackets, moved to the aft of the boat, slid the inflatable into the water, and snugged it to the *Voyageur II* with a line. "Get in," Evans commanded. Casperson stepped into the undulating craft and nearly pitched headlong into the lake when a swell slammed the Zodiac. "Careful, Casperson. Don't want to lose you too!"

Evans claimed the aft seat in the Zodiac and pulled the cord on a fifteen-horse Mercury four-stroke. The outboard purred. "Untie the line!" she yelled. Casperson complied and the inflatable drifted free. Beth Evans opened the throttle and turned the Zodiac into the waves. Within seconds, they were alongside the *Miss Sky*.

"He's gone, ma'am."

Evans bit her lip. Rain pummeled her face. Her raingear shed water as she surveyed the empty boat. "I can see that, Casperson." The woman scrutinized the *Miss Sky*. There were no plastic bins or wooden boxes full of herring in the skiff. *If he caught anything, it's long gone. Gull food by now. Shit. Sky is pregnant with their first. Goddamnit. The kid was pre-med. Granted, he knew ... strike that ... knows the lake. But goddamnit to hell, he had the world in the palm of his hand. Was gonna be a doctor. A medical doctor. And he drowns trying to bring in a few hundred dollars of herring? I just don't ...*

"There's something on shore!" Casperson yelled.

"Where?"

"Just south of the lighthouse, above the rocks!"

Evans steadied the Zodiac. The swells were flattening. The rain was diminishing. Beth Evans focused her attention on a body resting in thin grass. "Good eyes young man. Let's see if Kjell Thompson is still with us."

The *Voyageur II* chugged into the harbor. The storm was over. Night was emergent. Contact with the ranger station had been knocked out by weather. The Menagerie Island beacon was cycling as Everlasting Sky heard the tell-tale sound of marine engines, struggled from her chair, slid sandals over her swollen feet, and moved towards the front door. From the doorway Sky watched the *Voyageur's* spotlight illumine the dock, the fish house, and the sauna building. She gathered her courage and stepped outside wearing only a cotton nightgown.

Bang.

The screen door slammed shut behind her. The night air raised goose bumps on Sky's skin as she stood on wet lawn, her arms hugging her chest, and watched the boat settle alongside the Wright Island pier. The Ojibwe woman advanced no further: She was unable to accept what she believed to be the inevitability of her life.

But she was wrong.

Hannibal's Elephants

Last night I had that dream again. No, not the one featuring the pretty Hopi girl with the big brown eyes but the one about the Carthaginian general.

I am slogging through shin-high snow, one of nearly 40,000 men of Carthage and its Spanish allies marching towards Italy to confront the Romans. We are trying to cross the Alps after having crossed the Pyrenees in Iberia and the Rhone River in Gaul. Our objective is the plain of the Po River to the east of the mountains, which, if we are successful in finding a pass and descending from these snowy peaks, will open up Italy to our invading force like a compliant virgin spreading her legs. But goddamn it, this is brutal! It is cold. Even with heavy woolen cloaks sewn by Spanish women and purchased by our general—Hannibal Barca—at an outrageous premium and passed out to us, we are warriors from temperate North Africa and Spain. We are not adapted to winter, much less mountain climbing through snow. Our feet are covered in rags; our sandals having proven useless against the cold and wet. Our heads are bare. Our weapons conduct cold into our fingers whenever we are forced to handle them. Men are dying of disease and exposure and frostbite by the dozens every day. And then there are the animals. The horses and mules stay relatively warm with activity, though they too are near starving. Their hay and grain run short as we climb upward, always upward. But the elephants? We began the march with thirty-eight. All except Hannibal's personal mount, a small-eared animal of the Syrian sub-species gifted to our general by an Eastern potentate, are Atlas Mountain elephants from Morocco. Those animals are smaller, more compact versions of the large-eared African elephants associated with sub-Saharan forests and plains. But whereas Hannibal's personal elephant—due to being of the Asian variety, was easily trained and calm in battle— the Atlas elephants are fidgety, unruly, and difficult to manage. Still, it's a feat of history that we climb through the snows of the Alps behind a parade of elephants. If we make the Po River with one elephant left standing, our journey will be chronicled as miraculous, a story for the ages. But for now, we shiver, and cough, and listen to our empty stomachs as we climb towards the roof of the world accompanied by a concert of starving elephants.

Morning. I'm standing near the Russian border. It feels, as I try to recall *the* dream, as if I'm freezing to death, just like that Carthaginian warrior. But I'm not. I'm dressed for the weather, outfitted in winter camouflage provided by the United States Army, the white of my insulated uniform blending in with the flat, snowy landscape near Route 178 just west of Piussa Jõgi. I'm manning a checkpoint with other Americans dug into the frozen Estonian soil as part of a NATO exercise. I'm a captain, an officer of infantry. We've been deployed in an attempt to convince our Estonian allies—in this time of uncertainty—that our word means something; that the NATO treaty we signed and Estonia signed has legitimacy. It's been a long road for me. As a child, I did not yearn to become a soldier. I wanted to play point guard in the NBA.

My name is Augustus de Asis. I'm an Indian. American Indian from Taos Pueblo in New Mexico. I'm an accidental warrior, having stumbled into Army ROTC when I was playing ball for the University of Minnesota-Duluth. Duluth. Talk about cold! It snows at my Pueblo in New Mexico but rarely stays on the ground. Up in the mountains, where the rich people ski, sure, there's snow that stays all winter. But down in the valley by Taos and Santa Fe? Flurries come and go but nothing sticks.

As I stand here freezing my ass off, watching the maneuvers of the M1A Abrams tanks, M3AE Bradleys, and M1126 Strykers my detachment is supporting, Russian Army units doing nothing more provocative than assembling on their side of the border and watching us with keen interest, I think back to Hannibal and his elephants—the wondrous impossibility of it all. *What was that man thinking?* I begin comparing his journey—from North Africa to Spain to Italy and back, including his final battle defending Carthage against Scipio, the Roman general who eventually ended Hannibal's dreams and Rome's nightmare—with my own backstory. *Not nearly as interesting,* I admit.

I'm a ball player. My parish priest, Father Baraga, got me into DePaul on a scholarship. Pulled some strings. I was a skinny, undersized, Native kid who didn't belong in a D1 program. That became apparent when I stepped onto the court for my first practice. It wasn't like Coach Clinton, the head coach at DePaul, didn't see something in me. "You shoot a mean three, Geronimo," he'd say, watching me during practice. "But you're slower than a Chi-town gangster in cement overshoes." I didn't mind he called me Geronimo. I mean, despite the fact the storied warrior was Apache and not kin, he's still a hero to me. I admire the way he held out and tried to defeat the Blue Coats. *Against all odds, like Hannibal and his elephants,* I'd think, whenever Coach used that seemingly pejorative nickname.

The vision of Hannibal leading his army through the snowy Alps first appeared in my dreams after taking an ancient history class at DePaul during my freshman year, my only year at the Catholic school. My sophomore year, I found myself in Duluth. Coach Clinton took pity on my plight and found me a spot on a D2 team, the University of Minnesota-Duluth (UMD) Bulldogs. If I thought Chicago was cold—given the snow and wind coming off Lake Michigan—once I settled into a routine at UMD, where the campus overlooks Lake Superior, I became convinced that Minnesota is part of Canada. Thirty-two below zero actual one day in February is just plain insane.

I managed to adjust to the cold and the snow and the team and ended up being elevated to starting shooting guard, averaging just over twelve a game, mostly on threes. My junior year, I joined Army ROTC, accepting the money and the training the Army offered in return for a six-year commitment. That was ten years ago. I liked the discipline, the organizational structure, and the camaraderie of the military and decided to make the Army a career. Now, here I am, a company commander overseeing the deployment of American soldiers thousands of miles away from my ancestral home in New Mexico.

Looking across the river—watching the Russians shadow our maneuvers, contingents of German and Polish infantry guarding our flanks and providing additional protection for our armor, with jets and helicopter gunships from various NATO nations providing air support—*the* dream interrupts reality.

After a month of struggling to cross frigid, impossible mountains separating Gaul from Italy, we've crossed the Po and arrived on Roman soil. Though we're beleaguered—worn and tired and, having dwindled to less than thirty thousand men and having lost thirty of the thirty-seven elephants that began our ordeal—we remain undaunted, ready to avenge the countless injustices and humiliations the Romans have imposed upon our people over centuries of conflict. They said an invasion of Italy by land was impossible. That dream has become reality. We move forward, ready to do battle with a foe that vastly outnumbers us in a land we know little about.

    I scrutinize the buildup of Russians on the far shore of the Piussa and realize this truth: Just like the Romans, who rallied against Hannibal after a series of backbreaking and disheartening defeats, Putin's men will not yield. The Russians did not lose to Napoleon or Hitler and they will not lose to us. Just like the Romans taking Carthage, if the Russians want Estonia, they will have Estonia and anything else they deign to acquire. This realization doesn't, as one might suspect, cause me distress. Instead, I find the knowledge of Russian inevitability curiously comforting. Why this is, I cannot say.

    Tonight, I'll sleep soundly in my tent on the eastern plains of Estonia. I'll no longer dream of Hannibal and his long-suffering men because I've come to an accord with my fate and my obligation to serve. Instead of nightmares of cold, and frostbite, and dying elephants, I'll dream of a Hopi girl with infatuating eyes and offer a tenuous, selfish prayer to the Almighty.

Rain

Most people don't know anything about Kaua'i, the furthest west of the Hawaiian Islands. Its nickname is "The Garden Island." That's a fine label for a piece of lush, tropical, volcanic rock stuck in the middle of the Pacific but what you really need to know about Kaua'i is that it's prone to microclimates. It might be sunny on one side of the island and pouring buckets on the other. Usually, the rains are on the east side of mountains that make up the canyons and steeps of picturesque Waimea Canyon State Park, the Grand Canyon of the Pacific. Four hundred inches of rain a year fall on the top of the highest peak, Mount Wai'ale'ale. Hanalei, a town just east of the park near my apartment on the beach, gets a whopping seventy-eight inches of rain every year. My point here isn't to dwell on the island's weather. I just wanted you to know that most days, if rain is inundating Poip'u, just a few miles to the east in Lihu'e it can be bright and sunny, not a cloud in the sky. It's a crazy place to live in terms of moment-to-moment predictability, though; despite its crazed climate, Kaua'i's still pretty much paradise on Earth.

I don't live down south where most locals hang their hats. The southeastern coast is home to Kapa'a and Lihu'e, towns where nearly half the island's 50,000 souls live. Those residents are unfortunate. They live in close proximity to Lihue's port, where cruise ships dock and strangers disembark from impressively obnoxious ocean liners to buy sunscreen, bathing suits, and condoms (you never know who you'll meet on a cruise) at the town's Walmart. Like I said, I live in the north, away from people. It's a choice; a reasoned, thoughtful decision on my part. It's why I came to the island; a place as far away from the mainland as one can go and still be a full-fledged citizen of the United States.

It's raining again. Yesterday—Saturday—it poured. Six inches per hour and the rain still hasn't stopped. My girlfriend, Bonita, had to go out in this shit. She's a waitress at the Chicken Bucket in Hanalei. It's a couple of minutes by bike from my place to the drive-in. Nice, easy ride unless it's raining pitchforks. Which it was. Is. Bonita is also the night manager at that little piece-of-shit place. Makes just nine bucks an hour plus tips even though she has three girls working for her and has to close on Saturday nights. I've told her there's no need. I mean, I'm not rich but I have enough. I was a trial lawyer back in Minnesota for twenty years, a judge for another twenty before mandatory retirement at seventy pushed me out the door. Got a plaque stored in a box somewhere thanking me for my "dedicated public service" signed by the Chief Justice of the Minnesota Supreme Court, and a swift boot in the ass and that was that. But my state pension is damn good and I'm topped out on social security. I rent this place on the beach; a one-bedroom mother-in-law apartment in a house owned by the widow of a four-star admiral; a guy you've likely heard of but whose name I won't drop here.

My place is only seven hundred square feet but has its own kitchen, bathroom, sitting area, and the one bedroom. The house sits on stilts above some of the wildest surf in Hawai'i. Beautiful doesn't begin to describe the sunsets Bonita Juarez and I enjoy from the covered lanai that runs along the front of the house. The old widow's living quarters adjoin our flat and we share a common wall. The old lady hears everything that goes on in our place. Lord knows what she thinks, what with Bonita being only twenty-seven and a hell of a lot more energetic than I am!

When the ocean is calm, there's flat, open, golden beach as far as the eye can see. Just the sort of thing, along with a half Hispanic, half Japanese surfer chick girlfriend, an old man trying to write the great American novel needs for inspiration. I lucked out that day I flew into Seattle from Minneapolis, got stranded due to mechanical problems, stayed over, caught an early flight the next morning, and ended up sitting next to Bonita on the plane to Lihu'e. Or maybe it was Providence, right? Maybe it was something more fated than mere luck that put us side by side on that six-hour flight. Why such a young, beautiful, vibrant girl took an interest in a world-wizened, retired guy with a bad Minnesota tanning-bed tan and a gray ponytail tapping away on his laptop, time running short, a story needing telling, as we sat next to one another, made small talk, and sipped Coke over ice in those little plastic cups they give you on Delta flights, I have no idea. But she did. Show interest, I mean. And when it turned out she was headed to Hanalei to room with her older sister Abbie—married with two kids and a schoolteacher in the local elementary—I offered Bonita a ride in the old Jeep Wrangler I'd shipped ahead. Didn't matter that the cost of sending the Jeep across country to San

Diego, loading it on a freighter bound for Oahu, and ferrying the car by barge from Honolulu to Lihu'e was more than a year's rent. There was principle involved in having the Wrangler with me.

    Lois, my ex and the mother of our six kids, got everything else. All the stocks. All the bonds. The ski condo at Lutsen. The big house in Duluth perched high atop the ridge overlooking St. Louis Bay. The cabin in northwestern Wisconsin. Every stick of furniture and every piece of artwork. I got to keep my pension and social security, my fishing gear, my Browning over-under twenty gauge, my clothes, my books, my MacBook Air, and the Jeep. Lois even took possession of the kids—now adults—all of whom blame me for the breakup. Which, given I'd slept with Judge Thorsen's thirty-six-year-old court reporter, a divorcée with three small children who desperately wanted a wedding as the result of our four-month affair, was an extremely fair position for my four sons and two daughters to stake out. I've been on this island for three years, and so far, none of my kids have called me or written me or Facebooked me or texted or emailed me or Skyped me. I'm dead to them and my grandkids. For simply admitting that my marriage to their mother was over.

    I'm sitting on the lanai watching the sky open up. It's as if God has decided to empty all of the water evaporated throughout the world on this tiny hunk of rock. Rain spills over the eaves of this ramshackle house bypassing gushing gutters and downspouts to splat ten feet below the lanai and join an ever-growing freshwater lake threatening to isolate the widow's house from neighboring homes. She's here, the Admiral's wife is, hunkered down in her own space, saying the rosary—I'm pretty sure—since she's a devout Catholic who never misses mass at Saint William in Hanalei. I haven't checked on her since yesterday when the power went out and I fired up the old Honda generator the Admiral was smart enough to buy and have wired directly into the main electrical panel of the house. The Honda is purring away on a wooden platform beneath the deck. The widow's place is one of a half-dozen that has power thanks to the generator and a stockpile of plastic fuel cans filled with gasoline stored under the lanai. The Admiral was smart to plan ahead. Foresight: The man, a noted military strategist, had plenty of foresight. After I fueled and fired up the generator, I knocked on the widow's door and gave her my assessment. "It'll be OK," I said without much confidence. She'd nodded, thanked me, shut her door, and went back to staring out the big windows overlooking her section of the covered lanai, clearly worried about the crazy antics of the surf and the ever-growing lake surrounding her home. That was last night. Bonita should have been home by eleven: She never made it back.

    I'm worried about The Kid. That's my nickname for Bonita. She's forty years younger than I am and in fact, about the age of my youngest son. That was sort of what I was thinking when I struck up a conversation with Bonita on that Delta flight, *Here's just the girl for Robert,* I thought. *Smart, well put together, and witty.* I wasn't in the market to rob the cradle. But that's what happened once we settled in and she started asking me about my writing. I had to admit to her that, beyond publishing a few pieces of short fiction—contest winners though they were—in regional literary magazines and on writerly websites, I'm not famous. Or infamous. Or known beyond the small world of northeastern Minnesota. But she seemed intrigued by my attempt at late-in-life fame. I answered her questions, glanced at her left ring finger, and eventually offered her a ride to her sister's place in Hanalei. That's how it started. Talking on an airplane. A ride in my Jeep. Coffee at a local diner. Then sex in my rumpled queen-sized bed. A somewhat natural progression in human affairs.

    I don't want you to get the wrong idea. The Kid isn't some carnally starved creature seeking transitory thrills from strangers. She has a genuine heart and a genteel soul. But she is—despite being so small of stature she reminds me of a girl-blossoming-into-a-woman—an amazing lover. For one so young, I mean. Not that I know all that much. Beyond a few fumbling attempts at sex before I got married, there was Lois of course, and Stella, the court reporter. That's it. That's the sum total of my exploits as a man of the world. How many men Bonita slept with before I came along, I have no idea. Truth is, I don't care, though, from the way she figured me out, I'm pretty sure it was more than a few. Bonita fits my motto for life, something I came up with when trying to write with profundity: *Revel in the doing, in the journey, not the destination.* We don't talk about the future, The Kid and me. We just exist and live our lives day-to-day in paradise. Or at least we tried to until the rain.

    Morning comes and it's clear the widow can't go to Sunday mass even if the Catholic church is open. Which it isn't. The sky continues to weep. Rain thumps the steel roofing of the house, beating a deafening cacophony that drowns out thought. Rising water threatens the generator. I can't call Bonita because there's no cell phone service. I'm worried. The Kid should have been home before midnight. *I shouldn't have let her go out,* I think as I stand in the kitchen holding a cup of coffee, the benefits of having an alternative source of energy clear in the cup's comforting warmth. I have no idea where Bonita is. I think back to yesterday morning when she told me, when she showed me the results of the home pregnancy test she'd taken in the bathroom. The shock of realizing I was going to be a father again nearly thirty years after Lois was last pregnant hit me like storm surge crashing against a rocky point.

    I study the omnipresent rain, listen to the thunder, and watch lightning slash above the darkened landscape. For a moment, I think I might pray. I don't. I gave up on God, or rather, He gave up on me, a long time ago. Before Stella. Before my marriage to Lois went south. I can't exactly pinpoint when it was that the Big Fella and I parted ways. Or why. But we did. It wasn't an epiphany, a sudden turn of events that forced my hand. It was a gradual ebbing away of faith—like the inexhaustible waves eating at the sand beneath our lanai—that did in my belief. I stopped going with Lois to her quaint Evangelical church. Started watching CBS *Sunday Morning,* first with Charles Kuralt, then Charles Osgood, and finally Jane Pauley instead of listening to long-winded pulpitory pontifications. Until Bonita came along I'd lost faith in everything, including love. Then, The Kid gave me hope. *Gives me hope.*

    I watch rollers pummel boulders protecting the shoreline, the island's last buffer against the surging sea. I hear the generator sputter, then die. I climb down the stairs certain that the thing has run out of gas. It hasn't. I stand on the fifth step from the bottom and my toes are underwater. The Honda is submerged. The gas cans have floated off. The lights have gone out. Only muted, scarce daylight illuminates the world. I climb towards the widow's place to make sure she's OK. She is. She's dressed in her standard casual outfit, a designer pantsuit of muted pink, a scarlet scarf tied around her saggy, translucent neck, and white Sketchers without socks.

    "I'm OK, Bob," she tells me, her eyes betraying anxiety while she maintains calm, even speech. "Did Bonita make it home after work?"

I shake my head and stare at the roiling ocean, its normally blue and white froth frenzied to dirty brown. I know absolutely nothing of my girlfriend's whereabouts and don't know how to respond. The old lady touches my hand with bony, arthritic fingers. The white hairs of my wrist glisten from rain. Both of us are soaked to the skin despite being under the lanai's roof.

"I prayed," she says, the solemnity and authenticity behind her personal faith in God simple yet profound, "that she'll be alright."

Fifty inches of rain falls over the weekend. It isn't until Monday afternoon—around four o'clock—that a runabout carrying two Kaua'i County Deputies pulls up to the stairs leading to the lanai. I see the crumpled red and white Trek mountain bike stashed in the back of the boat, understand what the filled and zipped canvas body bag means, and don't need to hear what those men have to say.

Katydid

She walks along the beach, the surf crashing, the tremors of God's awesome power echoing across low, rolling dunes of golden sand. The girl doesn't walk alone. She has a friend, a boy, with her. The girl and the boy are on Waimea Beach—the beginning of miles of unbroken sand reaching from the town of Waimea to Polihale State Park. After entering the park, only a suggestion of a dirt track continues until it doesn't. When the road ends, the mountainous northwestern coast of the island is left to hikers and kayakers and boaters and wilderness campers.

Katherine Elizabeth Banes doesn't know these things. She has no idea of Kaua'i's geography. She possesses only a child-like comprehension of the changes that are occurring to her thirteen-year-old-body. In addition to entering adolescence, a confusing time for any child, Katherine—"Katy" for short—was born with Down Syndrome. Though perpetually stuck at the cognitive level of an eight-year-old, Katy is consistently and constantly in awe of her surroundings; every day a new adventure, every dawning sun, the beginning of a new escapade. Despite her limitations, the girl is kind and gentle and a lover of God. Her mother, Elizabeth, saw to that.

Katy's father, Edward, a tough, no-nonsense veteran of Desert Storm and a gunnery sergeant on active duty with the United States Marine Corps, seldom expresses softness or tenderness or the sort of parental nurturing a girl-turning-into-a-woman needs. But he cherishes his "Katydid," the pet name he adopted and applied to Katy when she was an infant struggling to nurse and emitting short, guttural, grasshopper-like sounds while rooting at her mother's breast.

"No one," Edward declared upon arriving home with his wife and their only child from a difficult Cesarean delivery, born when Elizabeth was nearly forty, the two parents believing that there was no hope of a pregnancy after years of barren love, "will ever call my daughter disabled. Or handicapped. Or retarded." The USMC lifer paused and nodded to his wife, her face pale, the cancer unknown but already blossoming, Elizabeth's blood surreptitiously carrying leukemia to the distant reaches of her body as she struggled to get Katy to latch onto her left nipple in the living room of their billet in San Diego. "If they do," Edward continued, "they'll have to deal with me," he said, holding up a mitt-sized right hand for emphasis, the knuckles calloused from years of hitting a heavy bag at the NCO gym. Elizabeth had smiled wearily but had said nothing. She knew her husband, knew he would—come hell or high water—protect their daughter from all slights and dangers and abuses the world might seek to inflict.

Elizabeth slipped away, her essence disappearing before Katy turned five, and the girl cannot comprehend the finality of her mother's death. She believes that, at any moment, Elizabeth may return. The child's sunny disposition persists despite her mother's demise; her perpetual happiness is buttressed by delusions of parental resurrection.

After Elizabeth's death, the child was mainstreamed in elementary school; the kindness and patience of teachers increasing tenfold towards Katy as a result of the tragic circumstances of her youth. She learned to read and write, though; given the totality of her limitations, it's unlikely she'll ever hold a job more taxing than working the end of a broom or a mop or a dishcloth. Katy's father realizes his daughter's vocational choices are destined to include work at sheltered workshops or other such charitable organizations established to provide pride and instill self-worth in young people like Katy. Edward grapples with this unfair reality. Given his stern and gruff persona, the result of being in combat and serving twenty-two years as a drill instructor, Edward is pessimistic about Katydid's future. But realist that he is, Gunnery Sergeant Edward Banes has a hard time letting fate and genetics and bad luck dictate his daughter's choices. He doesn't see the point of restricting Katy. Which is why, despite her innocent, sweet, completely trusting nature, she's walking Waimea Beach with a young man without adult supervision.

Edward and his second wife, Jill, are on their honeymoon. The tall, lanky, ponytailed, childless, Finnish Norwegian blond from Minnesota's Iron Range fell for the bulldog of a man with a crewcut while standing behind him in the checkout line at a San Diego Walmart. Beyond the love Edward feels for his new wife, it's Jill's complete and unadulterated acceptance of Katy that endears Jill to the taciturn Marine. She took to Katy as if the child were her own kin; completely and solidly enveloping the girl in a parental adoration so profound, it actually made the grouchy Marine—a dead ringer for the infamous fictional aviator Bull Meecham—smile. It was Jill who insisted that Katy come with the newlyweds on their honeymoon, though, for propriety's sake, this meant the sergeant had to spring for a two-bedroom cabin at the pricey Waimea Plantation Guest Cottages. Jill and Edward are discrete. Having been around the block, they're not overly demonstrative or vocal in expressing passion. All the same, Jill insisted that Katy have her own room given she was entering puberty and deserving of privacy.

It was Jill who explained—in the simplest of terms—to Katy what the cramping and the blood and the changes mean.

"You're growing into a woman, Katydid," Jill said earlier that day, the two of them sitting in the living room of the beachside cottage, Edward on a charter fishing excursion with other Marines who were staying in Navy-owned cottages at Barking Sands up the coast.

Edward had suggested that he and Jill save some dough and reserve a place at Barking Sands but Jill would have none of it. "You'll not cheat me out of a romantic getaway by trying to save a dime, Eddie. No way am I staying in some second-rate cabana." Truth is, the Barking Sands cottages are some of the most sought after vacation retreats owned by the military. But unwilling to engage in a skirmish with the woman he'd learned to admire, love, and entrust with his daughter, Edward caved, withdrew cash from his savings, and kept the peace.

Sergeant Banes was out, plying his luck on the charter boat from Port Allen when Jill explained the facts of life to the child and instructed her on the things all young ladies need to know to avoid embarrassment. The emergent reality of Katy's condition necessitated a trip to a convenience store to purchase items of a personal and, for the young Down Syndrome girl, somewhat perplexing nature. Jill was a patient and easygoing teacher and Katy ultimately understood what was required of her.

The child turning-to-woman is walking, waves crashing around her and her wheelchair-bound companion, boys and girls and men and women daring the surf on boards; some standing proudly against the late afternoon sun on short surfboards and riding waves until the sea's momentum withers in the shallows; others kneeling, making cuts and dashes on boogie boards atop powerful curls before overturning near the beach. As Katy and her the boy watch islanders and tourists play in the ocean, she believes she should be with them dancing atop the water, regaling in the wind and the solemn grace of motion. Though Katie knows how to swim, enough so to save herself if she falls out of a kayak—which she's done while paddling some nameless northern California river with other kids of her ilk from a camp Edward sent her to—she doesn't know the first thing about balancing on a board.

"I wish I could do that," she says to Ricky Lee, the boy she's with.

Ricky—the son of the caretaker of the Plantation Cottages—was born with spastic paraplegia. Ricky's legs have feeling but can't be controlled by his brain. His arms and hands are also unpredictable. Ricky rumbles along the randomly pitching beach, his right hand operating the joystick of his all-terrain wheelchair, the chair's wheels replaced by tracks akin to those on a bulldozer or tank; an alteration Ricky's father has made to the chair in the resort's shop.

"I wish Daddy would let me do that," Katy repeats.

"You'd be good at it," Ricky says. "Me, not so much!"

Katy giggles. She's wearing the new, one-piece bathing suit Jill picked out at a shop in Lihu'e. The suit—bright red with white flowers—is held up by thick straps across the girl's sun-reddened shoulders and covers Katy's prodigious rump; the fabric ending mid-thigh where Katydid's thick legs emerge from wide hips. The new suit also adequately—in her father's estimation—conceals the advent of breasts, reflecting modesty and dignity, traits Edward tries to instill in his child; traits Jill also emphasizes to Katy as a means of self-preservation. The reasoning behind Jill's cautionary tone is beyond the girl's ken: Katy is so trusting and open and naive, Jill fears a loss of Katy's innocence due to barbs and quips and comments and insults hurled by other children and unkind adults.

Still, Jill had thought as she watched Katy walk out the front door of the cottage to meet Ricky on the sidewalk, a lecture on safety and vigilance and personal awareness having been repeated before the girl and her friend left, the kids promising to be back before dark, *she must learn. What better place to do so than in the Garden of Eden?*

There'd been a flip of Katydid's chubby right hand before the girl's steady, deliberate gait moved her out of view. Ricky's chair was noiseless as it crept alongside Katy, the rubber treads leaving tracks in the sand as the kids embarked upon their adventure. Jill smiled thinking of the awe her stepdaughter and friend would behold when the big red sun slid behind the near-distant island of Niihau. There would be a moment of indecision as day slipped into night, the shoreline of Niihau becoming a pencil-thin line of finality just before the sun vanished. There would be enough light after sunset for the kids to find their way home. While Edward might have decided, had he been at the cottage and not drinking beer and fishing with his pals, to accompany Katydid and Ricky on their walk, Jill believed Katy deserved a moment of private discovery to understand, or at least, try to understand, her place in the world.

    Breakers are coming in hard against the rocks protecting Kikiaola Harbor, a small indention in the coast just north of Plantation Cottages. Phil Bradley sits on his surfboard, the only longboarder riding the waves this day; an old black man, his once tightly coiled ebony hair whitened by the passage of years and the Hawaiian sun. Phil's long, thin, arms and legs, leathery and sinewed from manual labor, dangle in the water. The old man's face is clean-shaven, "No sense adding more white to this old black skin," Phil is fond of quipping when he shows up at the barber in Lihu'e for his appointment, knowing any beard he might deign to grow would come out the color of winter. Despite being over seventy, Phil doesn't need contacts or glasses or cheaters. Clarity of vision and purity of heart are the old man's most admired attributes once he stopped drinking. But that metamorphosis occurred only after Phil's marriage, life, and world were shattered by an accident on the mainland that killed his wife and two of their three kids.

    Phil had been driving on the coastal highway north of San Francisco, missed a curve, and killed nearly everyone he loved because he was twice the legal limit. Six years in prison, complete ostracization from his surviving daughter—Emma, now forty-two—and the loss of his license to practice medicine followed. His time in prison? It sobered Dr. Phillip Bradley up: He hasn't had a drop in twenty-five years. But that doesn't matter a lick to Emma, now the mother of three herself and happily married to a brilliant man who runs some sort of IT company in Silicon Valley. Daughter and father haven't talked since Dr. Bradley went to the Big House and Emma went to live with his sister in Spokane.

Like so many who come to the farthest reach of Hawai'i, Phillip Bradley has remade himself. No longer Dr. Phillip Bradley but simply "Phil" Bradley, a proudly private black man with gleaming white teeth, perfect diction, and neatly trimmed nails; after arriving on the island, Phil found work at the Lihu'e Marriott as a groundskeeper. For nearly thirty years, even those closest to him on Kaua'i— including the three women he's lived with but never married—believe they are in the presence of a kind, hard-working man who has, at most, a high school education. No one, not even his current live-in, Lila Tuiasosopo, a fat, happy-faced, big-chested, Samoan woman who endured two bad marriages to two bad men and came to her relationship with Phil devoid of children, realizes that former groundskeeper Phil Bradley of Hanapepe, Kaua'i had once been Phillip Bradley, M.D., a renowned cardiac surgeon from San Francisco, California. Or, that before earning his BS from Stanford and his MD from Howard, Phil was a Marine grunt before becoming a Navy medic assigned to the Seals. Or, that as a medic, he'd been deployed with the Seals to Kosovo where he witnessed the ugliness of man's inhumanity.

Lila also doesn't know Phil used his GI Bill benefits to better himself, to become a first-rate heart man with a penchant for expensive Scotch and an unlimited ability to hide his drinking. It was only after tragedy that Dr. Bradley's secret came to light and he went to prison. That said, during his self-imposed exile on Kaua'i, Phil Bradley's criminal past hasn't been revealed to his fellow islanders or his live-ins. He's been on the cusp of telling Lila the whole sordid story. But the courage to come clean eludes him: He hasn't uttered a word about his past life in the military or as a heart surgeon or about the accident or the deaths of his wife and sons or his time in prison to anyone.

Phil faces the setting sun, breakers beating ragged against the stone barrier protecting the marina, sitting astride his longboard. It's an old board; a traditional koa wood surfboard with a single fin, varnished to sheen, heavy in the hands but elegant in the water. He traded a VW van, the engine blown but the body in good shape, for the board. Phil made that deal with an ancient Hawaiian who wanted to rebuild the Volkswagen and give it to his grandson. Phil has ridden the longboard for fifteen years and has never regretted the barter he made.

Phil scrutinizes the waves. Seeking the perfect ride to end his day, the old man exercises the same patience and prudence he once displayed in the OR. As he sits in contemplation, laughter reaches his ears. Phil turns his head to see a Hawaiian Monk seal, the endangered mammal having nestled in warm sand earlier that afternoon, sleeping on the beach despite the noise. He watches a short, dwarfish girl—her gait and arm swing clearly that of a Down Syndrome child—stop short of the seal as a boy operating a motorized wheelchair comes to rest beside her. There's no seal watcher—no volunteer whose job it is to prevent human-seal interactions—on the beach. Earlier in the day there'd been a volunteer sitting in a lawn chair protecting the animal but the seal guardian and her chair are nowhere to be found.

"Hey," Phil calls out in a fatherly voice, "you kids need to let that seal be!"

The girl looks at the black man on the surfboard, smiles, and waves. The boy in the wheelchair does likewise. The children heed Phil's admonition and do not advance. They remain a safe distance away from the Monk seal, studying it with innocent reverence, while to the west, the sun meets the horizon and flames the sky. Phil turns his eyes towards the ocean. As he does, he notes the shadowy silhouette of Niihau rising ghost-like from the plain of the Pacific and revels in the beauty of the world he's fled to. *I once thought that living here would be too claustrophobic, too confining,* he thinks. *But I was wrong about that, just as wrong as a man can be. But wrong too that isolation and deprivation from one's kind, the sort of internal penance I've manufactured here on Kaua'i, can end nightmares.*

Phil's time on the island has allowed him to reach a sort of stasis; he's placated but not eliminated his demons. *Maybe if I told Lila some of what it is that I'm running from,* Phil muses as a young native Hawaiian kneeling on a boogie board catches a wave and shoots past him, *some of my burden would lift. I doubt it. But it bears consideration ...* A large curl grows further out to sea. The old man ignores his troubles, turns his board, and claims it.

Phil Bradley stands on thin legs, his balance perfect, his heart racing. *This is gonna be one sweet ride!* Then, out of the corner of his eye, Phil sees the boy in the wheelchair gesturing wildly towards open water where the young woman, caught in the grips of a rip tide, is being dragged out to sea. Phil aims his board towards the stricken girl. When his wave is spent, the old man lowers himself to the deck and paddles like mad towards a mere speck of bobbing head and thrashing arms. And then, she is gone. Phil speeds to the spot on the vast, unfettered Pacific where he last saw the girl, unleashes himself from the board, and dives into the sea. He opens his eyes beneath the water's surface. Off Kaua'i, the water is clear and cold and the sea floor plunges towards depth. The west coast of the island is the habitat of deep water whales that hunt by sonar and great white sharks that cruise for prey. Phil is frantic. He knows the girl has little time. Precious moments pass. He sees nothing, resurfaces, gulps air, and dives again.

Phil beaches the longboard south of the marina. The boy in the wheelchair rushes to Phil's side, the treads of the motorized chair churning sand. The sky is nearly black. Only Venus is out when the old man comes ashore. Stars are not yet visible. The moon is absent. Boys and men and girls and women in swim wear and wetsuits who were in the water or walking the beach at the time of the girl's disappearance gather and stand vigil as Phil carries the girl in his arms, lays her on her left side, and thumps her back. Then just as he'd been trained to do, Phil Bradley begins chest compressions.

    The only thing Phil had been able to grab hold of as the girl sank towards the abyss—a flash of red visible as she descended—was a strap of the girl's bathing suit. He'd managed to grab one strap then the other, his lungs depleted, his muscles screaming for oxygen, before kicking powerfully to the surface. The left strap of the girl's suit ripped when Phil swung the girl's inert body onto his surfboard before paddling to shore.

    As he administers **CPR**, Phil doesn't worry that the girl's adolescent left breast and nipple are exposed to the night air and the curiosity of strangers. He ignores immodesty to save a life.

    "What the hell do you think you're doing?"

    An angry and threatening voice projects from behind the wall of onlookers. Phil doesn't reply. He simply continues the compressions.

    "Katy fell off the rocks," the boy in the wheelchair says through a crying jag. "I tried to tell her not to follow the seal, Mr. Banes, but she wouldn't listen."

An unfriendly hand grabs Phil's left bicep. "What the hell are you doing to my little girl?" the angry voice asks again.

Phillip looks up and focuses his coal black eyes on the man asking the questions; a military type pinching Phil's arm in a vice-like grip. A tall blonde woman with a ponytail stands next to the angry man and covers her face with her hands as she sobs.

"He's trying to save her life," a tiny, twenty-something Hawaiian girl in a form-fitting black wetsuit, a female surfer Phil knows only as "Maddie," offers. "He's giving her CPR. For God's sake, let him work!"

A white guy who'd been shore-casting for shark, a towering man in his early forties built like a professional football player, reaches in and breaks Edward Banes's grip. "He seems to know what he's doing. Let him be," the intervenor says.

Edward complies, steps back, and notices a tattoo on Phil's left arm.

"Semper Fi? You in the Corps?" Edward asks, harshness softened by recognition.

"Was. Transferred to the Navy. Became a medic," Phil says, his breathing labored from the rescue and doing CPR. "I went to medical school after Kosovo. Ended up a heart surgeon," he adds. *Shit. I've said too much.*

Before Edward Banes can reply, Katie coughs, spews water, and cries. Phil helps the girl sit up.

"Alright, Doc!" Maddie shouts.

Phil Bradley shakes his head. "I'm not a doctor anymore. Haven't been for years."

The girl wretches, vomits more water, but finally stops crying. Phil removes his hand and stands. Cheers and applause erupt from the crowd. Someone gives the blonde woman a beach towel. She uses it to restore modesty to Katy before subsuming the girl in a fierce bear hug. Hands are shaken. "Thank you's" are said. Folks disperse. The boy in the wheelchair, the girl, the father, and the tall blonde woman melt away, leaving Phil Bradley alone on Waimea Beach with his longboard to ponder whether it's time to tell Lila Tuiasosopo his secrets.

Crazy

You were sixteen. I was six. You were my big sister. Our brothers, Roger and Evan—identical twins—were away from home, attending Drake University in Des Moines. Roger was thinking of medicine. He ended up a dentist with a one-chair practice in Proctor. Evan got a business degree. Sells used cars in St. Cloud. You and I were still living at home when Dad died and Mom went crazy. You were only a teenager but, in less than a month's time, you became the head of our household.

Before it happened, you were a happy-go-lucky sophomore at Duluth Denfeld. I was in first grade at Laura MacArthur. Our house was on 47th and 8th in West Duluth. Dad, a Denfeld grad who grew up in the shadow of Public Schools Stadium—the football and soccer field located next to Denfeld—made sure we never uttered the trendy new moniker for West Duluth dreamed up by someone in the mayor's office, "Spirit Valley."

"It's West Duluth," Dad would mutter as he read the paper, pissed off about some article in which the *News Tribune* used "Spirit Valley" to describe his old stomping grounds. "It's not friggin' Spirit Valley. It's West Duluth!"

Mom, a traditional, stay-at-home mother of four, was just fine with Spirit Valley but never uttered the hated phrase within earshot of Dad. "I just don't know why he gets so upset about something so stupid," she'd say as we drove along Grand Avenue, you learning to drive behind the wheel of Mom's Accord, Mom next to you in the front passenger's seat, me buckled into the back seat. Mom would point out businesses and community buildings that had adopted the hated label, re-naming their buildings or organizations "Spirit Valley this" or "Spirit Valley that" and say, "Your Dad. He's so damn stuck in his ways. He's like Don Quixote jabbing his sword at windmills!"

You, of course, being older and having read the book for freshman English, got Mom's reference. Me, being mired in *Tip and Mitten* and *Jack and Jane* readers had no idea what our mother was talking about. But, and here's the thing: If the only point of discord in our home was Dad ranting about changing the name of our neighborhood, and Mom—who is from Superior, just across the Bong Bridge that towers above the St. Louis River, the river being the border between Minnesota and Wisconsin—didn't give a damn about whether she shopped in West Duluth or Spirit Valley, I'd say we were pretty lucky, Karen. Wouldn't you? At least from my perspective as the youngest Carver; me being ten years your junior and fifteen years younger than the twins, that's how I saw it. We weren't a perfect family but we came pretty close to the mark.

    When Dad fell off the DM&IR ore docks and landed on the frozen surface of the river sixty feet below the trains, after having forgotten to double-check the safety harness he was wearing to prevent his free-fall, that was the beginning of the end. You screamed when the police officer showed up at the door that Tuesday afternoon, Dad having gone to work before either of us was awake. No last goodbye kisses possible, no "I love you's" exchanged between daughters and father. He was there the night before, watching the ten o'clock news on KBJR and then, the next day, he was gone. We were both home from school when Officer Burns, one of the few black cops on the Duluth force showed up to give us the bad news. Mom wasn't home. She was at the West Duluth Branch of the Duluth Public Library picking up the latest Margaret Atwood novel. The lady cop came to the door and you screamed, began sobbing, and I, learning from you what had happened, joined in. Felicia Burns stayed with us, having notified the library that Mom needed to get home. Our mother walked in the back door, brushing new snow off her coat, and asked, "What's going on? The police called the library ..." She stopped in the archway between the kitchen and the dining room, saw the two of us sitting on the davenport wailing like lost kittens, noticed Officer Burns hovering over us like a black angel, recognized tragedy, and dropped her stack of borrowed books onto the hardwood floor with a thud.

    "No!" is all she said as she rushed to hold us. "Not Jim!"

    Officer Burns wanted to take Mom aside and tell her the details of what happened but Mom shook her head.

    "His girls were the loves of his life. They need to know."

    "But ma'am, the little one ..."

    Mom had shaken her head more emphatically and clutched me tighter, to where I could feel her breasts flatten. "They need to know. *She* needs to know."

From the officer, we learned how Dad died. How he thought he had the harness properly secured but how, when he leaned over a railing to check on the delivery chute—the big conveyor that sends taconite into the holds of the boats that carry ore down the Great Lakes—he slipped and fell, the unsecured harness trailing him like reins from a carriage team run amok. His partner, Gabe Larson, a guy who played poker and drank beer at the house with Dad and other guys from the docks, a guy who worked with Dad every single day, couldn't explain how Dad screwed up a routine procedure he'd done a thousand times.

"It just happened, ma'am," was the only explanation Officer Burns offered.

Mom's response to hearing the story was to hug us tighter and to cry harder. At six years old, I certainly didn't understand that such news could break her. She's a tough broad, having worked her way through college, UWS across the bridge, as a waitress in a grungy, decrepit strip bar—the Lamplighter. She earned her bachelor's in education with thoughts of becoming a teacher. But she ended up pregnant with the twins and had to marry Dad. Of course, these are not things I knew back then. You later told me the juicy details of Mom's story, putting her history, and what happened next, into perspective, including the fact she has nine younger brothers and sisters and that her own father, Grandpa Jack, left the family in the lurch—for one of the strippers at the Lamplighter, no less—a week after Grandma June had their ninth and last baby. At six, I had no perspective as to why Mom went nuts after Dad died. Maybe you, at sixteen, had a better understanding of what happened to Mom.

Mom's decline started after Dad's cremains were deposited in a columbarium drawer at Oneota Cemetery just up the hill from the house. Mom—with the help of her siblings and other relatives—kept it together through the service at Asbury Methodist, the luncheon in the church basement, and the inurnment. When the three of us were alone in the house the following evening, the twins having rushed back to school (I can't really fault them; it was exam week at Drake) it began. Again, because I was so young, I didn't notice something was up, but you did.

"Mom, is there anything I can get for you?"

You asked the question sitting on a chair next to our parents' bed, Mom's face buried in a quilt, her eyes vacant, her thin, auburn hair tied in a ponytail, her face wan and pale from crying and not eating for the better part of a week. I remember the exchange because I was right there, in my Toy Story nightgown, standing next to you. It was quiet in the house without Dad. No sounds of burping or farting or straining coming from the bathroom we all shared on the second level. No evidence of snoring emanating from our parents' bed. No outbursts about politics and the stupidity of "some people" bellowing from the living room as Dad watched MSNBC after I was in bed and you were doing homework in your room. Mom looked at you with those washed out, hazel eyes of hers, and shook her head.

It was the next day. You were in school, Geometry I think, when you got called down to the principal's office.

"Karen," Principal Nogorski said, "it's your mom. I'm so sorry."

"What is it, what's happened?" you asked, sitting in a chair across from Mr. Nogorski, thinking the worst, believing that God had somehow cruelly claimed our only remaining parent.

"She's at the Miller Hill Mall. Seems to be in a bit of a daze. Talking gibberish and not at all oriented to where she is," the principal said. "She's in the security office. She apparently tried to take some items from Younkers without paying for them."

"Oh God!"

You told me later that the principal was very empathetic. He walked around his desk and hugged you. "It's not serious. The store's convinced she didn't know what she was doing. They're not calling the police. But she needs someone to take her home."

You nodded, sat in the school office in silence, thinking how you could make it to the Mall since Mom had the Accord and Dad's F-150 was in the garage.

"Mrs. Smith—your guidance counselor—will give you a ride."

You told me that when you picked Mom up from Younkers, she was disheveled, hadn't taken a shower, was wearing the same clothes she'd had on the day before, hadn't put on any makeup, and hadn't bothered to brush her hair. You said, after I got home that afternoon from school that "Mom's a mess. She's had some sort of nervous breakdown or something."

Her behaviors became more and more erratic. She started believing that the law required drivers to only make right-hand turns. She insisted upon eating Lucky Charms every morning but only if the marshmallows were removed and burned. Not tossed in the garbage. Burned. "They're filled with cyanide, you know," she would say as she plucked weirdly shaped bits of marshmallow out of her cereal bowl, place them in an ashtray, douse them with lighter fluid, and hold a cremation of magically delicious shapes right there on the kitchen table. I only saw the half of it. You saw, and had to deal with, much more. Her sending off check after check after check to Sunday morning televangelists until we were in jeopardy of losing the house because, while she had no trouble funding God's work, she couldn't seem to pay our bills. Her lining a ball cap with tin foil to "keep the government, the ones who killed James" from reading her thoughts and directing her to do evil. You saw it all and—God bless your soul—realized Mom needed help. But before you could get her in to see her doctor at St. Luke's, the Duluth hospital covered by our medical insurance, the shit hit the fan. A month of her craziness, you being dog tired and barely able to go to school—concerned about leaving Mom alone in the house to do God knows what to the place—and it finally happened. The straw that broke the camel's back.

"I'm afraid it's your mother again, Karen," Officer Burns said as the two of you sat in the West Duluth Police Station after you were summoned there by the cops. This time, you didn't need a ride. You'd started driving Dad's truck to school, saving me a bus ride by dropping me off at Laura MacArthur and then driving yourself to Denfeld.

I've imagined your face a hundred times as you listened to Officer Burns relate the details of why you were being called out of class. You weren't surprised. You'd had a month of bizarre to deal with. Uncle Steve, the next in line in Mom's family in terms of age, got Mom to agree to make the two of you Powers of Attorney and have your name added to Mom's bills and accounts. A lot for you—at sixteen—to handle, I know. But damn, Sister, you did it! You were managing our family affairs and keeping Mom out of trouble up until that visit to the West Duluth Police Station.

"What did she do now?"

Officer Burns sat back in her chair and shook her head. "It's bad, Karen. Really bad."

I don't know what sort of thoughts went through your mind before the officer related what had gone on. Did you, for example, think Mom had taken her own life? Or, more likely, did you believe she'd fallen victim to the paranoid delusions of evil that increasingly seemed to be her focus, perhaps acting out and attacking someone with violence? Maybe killing an innocent stranger?

"What did she do?" you asked again.

"She was found in the nursery of St. Mary's hospital, naked as a jaybird, her clothes neatly folded and stacked on a chair, with a newborn in her arms. She was standing in the nursery in the altogether, holding a baby girl, trying to get her to breastfeed."

"Oh my God!"

Officer Burns (as you relate the story) nodded and said the obvious: "She's out of control. She needs to be seen by a mental health practitioner. Likely needs strong medications."

I'm guessing that you nodded; the sadness and depth of what was transpiring, the loss of Mom as we knew her, covering you like a funeral pall. "Where is she?"

"At St. Mary's ER. They brought her down from the nursery. She's in one of the triage rooms, sedated. She became combative when a nurse tried to take the baby from her. Staff had to give her a hypo to retrieve the infant."

I know now how smart you are. Right then, at sixteen and confronted by disaster, your brain began to work it out. "I've got Dad's truck. I can pick up Susie from elementary school and then deal with Mom."

Which is exactly what happened. But there was a glitch. Dad's medical insurance, which, through Social Security survivors' benefits, worker's compensation, and savings, you and Uncle Steve were able to keep in place, paid full coverage but only if the medical facility was "in network." Our network was St. Luke's, not St. Mary's-Essentia. Which meant there was a problem when you and I showed up in the St. Mary's ER.

"What do you mean, the psychiatrist won't see her and evaluate her?"

I remember that was your response when we were told we needed to move Mom from St. Mary's to St. Luke's. You were pissed. Even a kid could see that.

"I'm sorry, Miss Carver, but he's extremely busy. And your coverage is only 50% out of network," the officious, twenty-something young, female billing clerk said as we sat in her cubicle trying to sort it all out before seeing Mom. "You'd be better served by transporting her to St. Luke's and have the staff there evaluate her."

I learned some bad words that day.

"Fuck that. My mother is sick, goddamn it. Our father is dead. She's all we have. I'm sixteen and this little girl, Susan, is only six. She made a scene in your hospital, somehow got the idea that the baby in the nursery is hers ..." You took a breath then, gritting your teeth and pointing your finger at the young lady, "... proving she's desperately sick. I'm not leaving. She's not leaving. We're not leaving. Not until a fucking psychiatric nurse or doctor evaluates her and gives her medication to control whatever it is that's going on inside her brain!"

We sat for two hours on plastic chairs in the little room where Mom was sleeping, her breathing labored due to the Haldol they'd pumped into her, the curtain closed to the hustle and bustle of the ER. A doctor finally showed. What I recall is that Dr. Godfrey—Emmit I think is his first name—didn't take exception to your insistence. In fact, he applauded your courage and resolve. Despite him being out of network, you ended up hiring him to be Mom's psychiatrist.

"I'm thinking schizophrenia. But here's the thing," the smiling, tall, thin, balding doctor said through full lips, his green eyes dancing as he talked to us like we were adults, "it's pretty unusual for the disease to manifest," he paused to ensure I understood that word, "that is, 'show up,' at age forty-three. All the signs point to schizophrenia, which, if untreated, is a horrific disease but which, if properly managed, can be arrested to allow your mom a decent life." He then placed his narrow, long fingers on Mom's right wrist—not as part of an examination, but as a gesture of kindness. "I'd like to get some other folks in here to consult, keep her a few days, try some things, and hopefully, avoid any more incidents like what took place upstairs."

Mom went on Zyprexa. You know that because you're the one, ten years later, still taking care of the details. And, true to his word, Emmit Godfrey has remained Mom's psychiatrist despite our insurance only paying half his fee. Mom's okay with paying the rest out of pocket. She's still not the feisty, hell-bent-for-leather young mother we had before Dad died. And she still has bouts of depression and sadness when she dwells on what happened. But damn it girl, you did good. You stood your ground that day in the ER, got Mom the help she needed, and today, even though things aren't perfect, they're pretty good.

You've sacrificed a lot. Despite getting pregnant at seventeen—by a guy you had no interest in marrying—and becoming a mom at eighteen, you stayed home to raise me and keep an eye on things. I'm grateful for that, Big Sister. I'm now at the age you were when this whole sorry mess began and more fully appreciate what you've done.

I love you for it.

The Last Jew

Yesterday there were two. Today there is only one. Her name is Frieda Rosenbaum Neumann. She is ninety-seven years old. Frieda was born in Virginia, Minnesota in 1921 to Jacob and Ada Rosenbaum; Jews who immigrated to Minnesota from Germany in 1919. When I say that she is the last one, I mean Frieda is the last Jew living in Aurora, a sleepy little taconite mining town located on the far eastern edge of the Mesabi Iron Range in northern Minnesota. Up until yesterday, there were two; two Jews living in Aurora—Frieda and her daughter Deborah. Deborah died yesterday. Frieda still manages her own household but how long, given her age and infirmities, will that go on now that her daughter has passed?

When the Rosenbaums arrived in Virginia there were enough Jews in town (and in the adjacent towns of Gilbert, Biwabik, and Aurora) to support a synagogue: B'nai Abraham. Hibbing and Chisholm to the west, and Eveleth to the south also had vibrant Jewish communities but, whereas B'nai Abraham in Virginia and B'nai Zion in Chisholm constructed their own temples, the Jews in Hibbing and Eveleth converted existing Christian church buildings into Jewish houses of worship. The Rosenbaums were less than rigid in their faith, worshipping at B'nai Abraham in Virginia on an infrequent basis. But whereas Jacob and Ada—and their two daughters, Frieda and Esther—were at best occasional congregants at the Friday Shabbats conducted at B'nai Abraham, they were most assuredly Jewish in culture and habit. Part of the Rosenbaums' identification as Jews—in the maelstrom of nationalities and cultures that swirled through the Iron Range as a result of immigration from the Balkans; Finland; England; Ireland; Norway; Sweden; Germany; Poland; and a host of other European countries—was dictated by the family's vocation.

Jacob, the patriarch of the family, and his son-in-law, Frederick Neumann—Frieda's "lazy, good-for-nothing-bastard of a husband" (to use Nana Ada's endearment for the man)—owned and operated a string of retail storefronts, each of which included a full deli, grocery section, bakery, and butcher shop. At the peak of the family's prosperity there were Rosenbaum Grocery Stores in Virginia, Gilbert, Biwabik, and Aurora. The family business puttered along until Jacob passed away on December 8, 1961, the day his heart, without warning or premonition, stopped.

"That," Nana Ada lamented, looking over the books of the tidy empire her husband had bequeathed to Frederick as the only remaining male in the family, Frieda having birthed only Deborah as offspring of the Rosenbaum line, Aunt Esther being covertly lesbian and having left the Range for Chicago years earlier to live with a young, female artist, "is that. Kaput."

The old matriarch's remark was uttered in 1973 when the last store, the Aurora location, was shuttered due to Fred's inability to keep a checkbook. "I told Jacob when he brought that boy in as a store manager that Fred would be the ruination of us." Ada had paused as she made an accounting of the business, penciling in the debits and credits that revealed another year of loss and the steady depletion of the family's savings. "And he was."

The buildings were sold and the sales generated enough cash—ahead of the downturn in the mining economy that gutted the Mesabi Iron Range in the early 1980s—for Ada to buy a small house in Virginia and for Frieda and Fred to buy a place on Colby Lake in Hoyt Lakes. Ada remained perfunctorily active at B'nai Abraham through her death in 1982, dying just before the synagogue closed; the number of Jews on the Iron Range having been diminished with sincere finality by the shuttering of the taconite mines and processing plants due to a lack of a demand for steel.

Fred ran off with a younger woman just before Ada's death, though the exact date of the end of the marriage was not something Frieda memorialized. Fred took everything the couple had in their bank accounts and, as trustee for the trust account Ada had set up for her one and only grandchild, Fred also embezzled everything Deborah was entitled to when she came of age. Cleaned out, left "without a pot to piss in," Frieda was fond to tell anyone within earshot. Once her "lazy bastard of a husband" vamoosed, Frieda sold the house on Colby Lake (she wasn't a country person and never learned to enjoy rural living) and bought a little bungalow on 2nd Avenue North in Aurora.

Deborah graduated from the College of St. Benedict in St. Joseph, Minnesota, moved to the Twin Cities, married twice, divorced twice, and, like Aunt Esther, remained childless. In Deborah's defense, it wasn't as if she didn't want kids. She was, to use her mother's words, "barren and bereft." Deborah's infertility was the major reason the only child of Frieda and Frederick Neumann endured two divorces. Both of Deborah's husbands wanted kids and both decided to pull the plug when the big event couldn't happen.

"I have the extra bedroom, you know," Frieda said when Deborah visited Aurora after retiring from the Teacher's State Bank of Anoka. Deborah had accepted a low-paying, entry-level teller's position to "get her foot in the door" after she graduated from St. Ben's. She ultimately kicked the door wide open and climbed the corporate ladder to become the bank's president, earning a mid-six-figure salary and enjoying generous profit-sharing and bonuses at the time of her retirement.

They were sitting and visiting in the kitchen of Frieda's two-story—the gray haired matriarch, her body shriveled from age to mere silhouette, her chin sagging, her bulbous nose interrupted by coarse white hairs that Deborah desperately wanted to pluck, Frieda sipping cheap Merlot while Deborah fidgeted with a tumbler of Bombay and ice—when Frieda made the offer. It was not a casual conversation. Anxiety and dread and sadness permeated the kitchen. The scent of freshly baked German rye bread, Jacob Rosenbaum's specialty, wafted from the oven as Deborah studied her glass of gin and ice and nodded. "I think that would be fine, Mother," she whispered. Though Deborah fought back tears, Frieda could see her daughter's eyes were moist. "I'd like to come home."

"I understand."

"There's nothing left for me in Anoka. I'll put the house on the market. It'll sell quickly given its location and the remodeling I've done. I bought Evan out years ago and I've paid down the mortgage. It's all equity. Whatever I get for the place goes into savings."

"Good. You'll need that for your treatments and, hopefully, for a trip or two once you're in remission."

Their conversation, one in which Frieda assumed that healing for her daughter was possible, had been based upon a lie. *Mother cannot know,* Deborah thought, as they made their plans to renew a life together. *She would collapse in grief right here, right now if she knew it was ALS instead of cancer.*

Deborah—in her sixty-seventh year and having reclaimed her maiden name Neumann—was eventually forced to admit her lie. That conversation, held in the White Community Hospital Nursing Home where the former banker came to spend her final days—home

151

hospice not being an option given the complete shutting down of her mobility and her ability to swallow and breathe—had been excruciating.

"Daughter, why did you lie to me? Why?" Tears had soaked the housedress Frieda wore draped over her narrow shoulders. The old woman owned a dozen nearly identical dresses and wore a version of the same dress every day. Deborah had never seen her mother wear slacks, shorts, or a bathing suit. Even when Frieda and Fred lived on Colby Lake, the old woman's clothing habits never wavered. Her dresses are her uniform; the housedresses in faint calico prints were something expected, and to the stricken woman, somehow comforting. Frieda had been holding her daughter's withered, inert right hand as she asked the question.

Deborah had lost the ability to speak except through an electronic device. Unnatural, Stephen Hawking-like speech leaked out as Deborah puffed on a straw: "I don't know. I guess I didn't think you could handle the truth."

Frieda had nodded but said nothing. Mother and daughter sat together in the antiseptically forlorn room, the gloaming of a winter's day casting shadows across cheerily painted powder blue walls, the last of their kind living in Aurora, Minnesota; their love evident, Deborah's passing, imminent.

About the Author

Mark Munger, a former trial attorney and District Court Judge, is a lifelong resident of Northeastern Minnesota. Mark and his wife, René, live on the banks of the wild and scenic Cloquet River north of Duluth. When not writing fiction, Mark enjoys hunting, fishing, skiing, and reading excellent stories.

Other Works by the Author

The Legacy (ISBN 0972005080 and eBook in all formats)
    Set against the backdrop of WWII Yugoslavia and present-day Minnesota, this debut novel combines elements of military history, romance, thriller, and mystery. Rated 3 and 1/2 daggers out of 4 by *The Mystery Review Quarterly*.

Ordinary Lives (ISBN 97809792717517 and eBook in all formats)

Creative fiction from one of Northern Minnesota's newest writers, these stories touch upon all elements of the human condition and leave the reader asking for more.

Pigs, a Trial Lawyer's Story (ISBN 097200503x and eBook in all formats)
    A story of a young trial attorney, a giant corporation, marital infidelity, moral conflict, and choices made, ***Pigs*** takes place against the backdrop of Western Minnesota's beautiful Smoky Hills. This tale is being compared by reviewers to Grisham's best.

Suomalaiset: People of the Marsh (ISBN 0972005064 and eBook in all formats)
    A dockworker is found hanging from a rope in a city park. How is his death tied to the turbulence of the times? A masterful novel of compelling history and emotion, ***Suomalaiset*** has been hailed by reviewers as a "must read."

Esther's Race (ISBN 9780972005098 and eBook in all formats)
    The story of an African American registered nurse who confronts race, religion, and tragedy in her quest for love, this novel is set against the stark and vivid beauty of Wisconsin's Apostle Islands, the pastoral landscape of Central Iowa, and the steel and glass of Minneapolis. A great read soon to be a favorite of book clubs across America.

Mr. Environment: The Willard Munger Story (ISBN 9780979217524: Trade paperback only)
    A detailed and moving biography of Minnesota's leading environmental champion and longest serving member of the Minnesota House of Representatives, ***Mr. Environment*** is destined to become a book every Minnesotan has on his or her bookshelf.

Black Water: Stories from the Cloquet River
(ISBN 9780979217548 and eBook in all formats)
    Essays about ordinary and extraordinary events in the life of an American family living in the wilds of northeastern Minnesota, these tales first appeared separately in two volumes, *River Stories* and *Doc the Bunny*. Re-edited and compiled into one volume, these

are stories to read on the deer stand, at the campsite, or late at night for peace of mind.

Laman's River
(ISBN 9780979217531 and eBook in all formats)

A beautiful newspaper reporter is found bound, gagged, and dead. A Duluth judge conceals secrets that may end her career. A reclusive community of religious zealots seeks to protect its view of the hereafter by unleashing an avenging angel upon the world. Mormons. Murder. Minnesota. Montana. Reprising two of your favorite characters from *The Legacy*, Deb Slater and Herb Whitefeather. Buy it now in print or on all major eBook platforms!

Sukulaiset: The Kindred
(ISBN 9780979217562 and eBook in all formats)

The long-awaited sequel to Suomalaiset: People of the Marsh, Mark Munger's epic novel of Finnish immigration to the United States and Canada, *Sukulaiset* portrays the journey of Elin Gustafson from the shores of Lake Superior to the shores of Lake Onega in the Soviet Republic of Karelia during the Great Depression. The story unfolds during Stalin's reign of terror and depicts the interwoven lives of Elin, her daughter Alexis, an American logger, and two Estonians wrapped up in the brutal conflict between Nazi Germany and Communist Russia. A page-turning historical novel of epic proportions.

Boomtown
(ISBN 978-0979217593 and eBook in all formats)

An explosion rocks the site of a new copper/nickel mine in northeastern Minnesota. Two young workers are dead. The Lindahl family turns to trial attorney Dee Dee Hernesman for justice. A shadowy eco-terrorist lurks in the background as Hernesman and Sheriff Deb Slater investigate the tragedy. Are the deaths the result of accident or murder? Equal parts legal thriller and literary fiction, this novel reprises many characters from Munger's prior novels. A page turner of a tale.

Kotimaa: Homeland
(ISBN 978-1-7324434-0-2 and eBook in all formats)

Wondering why Anders Alhomäki, the protagonist in *Suomalaiset* left Finland as a young man? How does the historic migration of Finns from Nordic Europe tie into the present-day immigration of Muslim refugees to Finland? Is a terrorist's threat on the cusp of Finland's centennial real or imagined? Part historical novel, part contemporary thriller, this book is the culmination of more than fourteen years' research. The final chapter in Munger's Finnish trilogy, *Kotimaa* is certain to challenge and entertain!

Visit us at:
www.cloquetriverpress.com
Shop at our online store!

10% of all gross sales of CRP books are donated by CRP to SmileTrain in hopes of helping children born with cleft lips and palates across the world. Learn more about SmileTrain at http://www.smiletrain.org/.